DISCO
DEATH

BY CHARLENE TORKELSON

Copyright © 2011 Charlene Torkelson
All rights reserved.
ISBN: 0615487912
ISBN-13: 9780615487915

This book is dedicated to all the dancers I have met, all the dancers I have danced with, and all those I have taught. In some form or another you are a part of this book. A piece of you is in each and every character and in each dance performed. You are a special group of people with unique talents. You have and always will be a part of my life. Since the first year I began ballroom dancing, I have worn a small gold band on my little finger signifying my dedication and connection to all the dancers in the world. This book is for all of you who have played such a significant role in my life. Thank you.

DISCO DEATH

Introduction:

Christmas 1977. John Travolta strutted his stuff across the movie screen in "Saturday Night Fever", and suddenly the dance world would never be the same. People of all ages began to flock to little hole in the wall studios to learn the latest "touch dances". Every night they crowded the discos that began to pop up to watch and maybe attempt the smooth Swing Hustle or the dramatic Tango Hustle under the spraying flashes of the twirling disco ball that circled above every dance floor.

The polyester revolution had begun. Men wore colorful open necked shirts with rings of chains and high stacked shoes. Women put on clinging leotards wrapped in slit skirts and tied their permed hair on top of their heads into "disco tails". It was an abrupt change from the frumpy long skirts and peasant blouses of the flower children. No longer the unkempt hair flying out from a pale face, the disco era brought on a slick heavily made up look that exemplified the flashy new dances and showy manner of the accomplished dancemasters.

Minneapolis was no stranger to the new trends. A cozy dance studio tucked beneath a stacked parking lot in downtown became the new haven for anyone who wanted to travel with the Travolta crowd. Young teachers and students began to frequent the domain of dancemaster Edward Garrett. His original choreography and charismatic personality drew the rich and the want-to-be with-it elite of Minneapolis and St. Paul. It also brought about his demise.

I.

Sydney Monroe lightly stepped off the bus into the mayhem of the city. At nine AM the commuter business people had already buzzed into their monthly parking spots and disappeared into their high rise cubicles. The night people and the homeless weren't out yet, so the clapboard of street construction seemed gloomy and deserted.

Her taupe raincoat billowed behind her as she crossed the street. She tugged on her hood to hide her face from the whip of the early morning wind and passed the three story parking ramp on her left before turning into the descending walk ramp. At the bottom of the ramp was an elevator to the layers of the parking area and to the right the door to a dance studio. Oddly, the glass front shadowed only by a filmy curtain showcased a circular reception desk and a gleaming wooden floor lined with mirrors. The prints of curiosity seekers lined the glass at eye level.

Sydney pulled on the door. Locked. She leaned against the wall and waited - only occasionally peering in. Practice started at 9:15, but no one ever arrived on time. It was pointless she knew but old habits die hard, and she had always lived her life being too punctual. With a sudden flick, the lights inside startled her although she was expecting them. The sweeping shadow of a man put a key in the lock and quickly vanished. Stepping inside, she shivered. It was colder inside than out. She hung her coat on the makeshift rack pushed back into the corner and ventured out to the floor. She blew warmth into her chilled hands as she hunched on the floor in a modified straddle position.

The tiny tinkle of a bell on the door announced the arrival of a fellow dancer. Amanda Garrett floated in wrapped in an ankle length fox fur. She stood momentarily on the carpet that divided the reception area from the dance floor. She smiled and nodded a greeting before turning toward the closed door behind her. The door closed off the office of studio owner Edward Garrett. His floor to ceiling glassed sanctuary was heavily draped with curtains hiding the beautiful mahogany desk and thickly padded chairs Sydney had only briefly glanced at as she passed the door. Only the special elite were invited into that office. All women of course. Amanda was Edward's wife – rumors had it soon to be ex-wife. She was always allowed into the inner sanctions of that space. A top model, Amanda Garrett was tall and thin but with a strange exotic and Bohemian air. Although wrapped in an elegant fur coat, underneath, Sydney was sure she wore torn dance tights and layers of stretched out sweaters. Amanda's hair was piled on top of her head in a curly puff with a few straggling hairs wisping around her face and neck. She was always kind. That's a subtle way of saying she didn't act like a model. Amanda Garrett had a kindness about her that was Mona Lisa-like in mystery — aloof, yet that slight smile and earnest gaze gave the space around her a feeling of calm and warmth.

Amanda came in first just as Sydney had predicted with heavy socks over her tights hiding the holes cut with a dull scissors at the toes and heels. She smiled that tight lipped grin and asked how she was today. "Fine," Sydney replied.

Edward Garrett followed – long striding steps in bare feet, tight dancer pants, a sleeveless leo, and a wool cap pulled down over his eyebrows. His presence was like that of a tornado – full of energy and hyperactivity. The cap covered a balding head that was normally topped with a curly toupee. Those close to him often compared him without his hair to Howdy Doody – a round freckled face with chipmunk cheeks and mouth like a cartoon character. This morning that mouth was pressed into a scowl. He forcefully pulled his hat down around his ears, glared into the mirror, and propelled over to the sound system. He snatched up a favorite piece of music and turned on the system. Then in a loud blast, he cranked up the music and took his place next to Amanda. Without saying a word to anyone, he began feverishly warming up with his usual routine. Amanda waited for one run through and then joined in as did Sydney. It would take a few minutes for Edward Garrett to become human. He was definitely not a morning person, but his fears of aging and fat were more powerful than his dislike of the early hours. The dancing and music would soothe the savage beast in him so to speak.

Eddie G., as people called him behind his back, owned this studio and the people in it. He was about as eccentric as a person could be. In one moment he could make you furious, the next he had you laughing at his crazy antics. He could be oozing with charm and complimentary, or raging and ... well, raging is the best word to describe Eddie G. Edward and Amanda were like oil and water, salt and pepper, hot and cold.

Not a word was spoken. The music blared through the room hiding the tinkling of the bell on the door. Sydney could see faint movement in the mirror. Several tall models sauntered in. Unlike Amanda, these women definitely had an attitude. Suddenly, Edward's face lit up. "Good morning, ladies," he boomed pulling his wool cap down to his ears again. His grin spread across his face and his arms and legs began pumping even harder than before. Amanda's small sweet smile never changed. The women took their places on the floor in a prominent place before the mirrors. Tossing their long hair back, they took a moment to gaze at their reflections. Edward chatted away with his usual babble, singing the words to the song, and getting funky with his moves.

Two men entered from the back side of the reception area. One Sydney knew was a model. His dark hair and toned body contrasted to his nondescript personality. The other one was another dancer who taught lessons at the studio with Sydney. Antoine Hawks could have passed for another male model. His outgoing manner endeared him to all who met him. Amanda turned around for a moment to acknowledge his presence. They seemed to send an electric charge across the room for that split second. It made Sydney think. She knew Antoine was gay. He made it very clear to everyone who knew him beyond the front desk business atmosphere the studio offered students.

A down home country boy, Antoine Hawks real name was Anthony Hawkinson. Sydney had seen the evidence on his driver's license when he was carded while writing a check for his lunch. She asked and he told. When he left the farm, Anthony disappeared and Antoine was born. He still held that face that every mother couldn't get enough of and possessed the talent and charisma that would make him successful in whatever he tried. This connection to Amanda Garrett was a mystery to Sydney. She shook it off and struggled with her conditioning.

Edward Garrett's morning exercise classes lasted forever. When he was in town, teachers and model friends could count on a class every day, seven days a week. He was so obsessed with himself, that Edward plodded on with his exercises and unique choreography for several hours until it was time for the normal dance business day to begin around one o'clock. The more people in the session, the more Eddie G. was inspired to keep going. This was his show, and he knew it. One by one, people began to leave as their schedules called and their bodies tired.

Sydney was stuck. No place to go except to the back teacher's office. She could hide out for a while before the daily meeting and dance session. The teacher's office was in stark contrast to the plush office Edward Garrett occupied. The back room was really a big old furnace room complete with a big boiler in the back corner and old worn, ripped carpet that seemed to trip her every time she walked through. No windows, no fresh air, the room possessed a heavy dark spirit tinged with the smoke left from the day before from those who still couldn't kick the cigarette habit. Two big old desks were pushed to each back corner for the "executive" branch of the staff. No one wanted the promotion to executive. It was filled with hours of meetings with Edward Garrett – his tantrums and his endless babble about a new idea to expand business. Whether it was sending teams of dancers to cruise ships or opening a tropical club, nothing ever amounted to anything more than just an idea. No, the executive positions were not charming.

Sydney settled into a folding chair after stripping off her leotard and slipping on her skirt and sweater. She lined up her few pairs of dance shoes in the small space designated as hers. The room was dark. The door opened. Suzanna Caldwell bustled in carrying a stack of papers and wrapped in an emerald cloth coat and scarf. She plopped her papers and purse down on one of the back desks and peeled off her damp coat. Quickly lighting up a cigarette, she slumped in her chair.

"Oh, my god," she gasped almost losing the cigarette from her mouth. "I didn't see you sitting there." She laughed and leaned back in the ripped padded desk chair. "Come in for exercise class? I don't know how you can do it. Eddie G. is such an obsessive fanatic about his fitness routine. He would drive me crazy."

Suzanna was the Supervisor and Manager of the studio. Her years with Edward Garrett had been many. A beautiful dancer, Edward had never given her the credit she deserved for her talent not only in dancing but with people. She was a tiny lady with a bird like face. Large round glasses perched on her nose and straight cut bobbed hair gave her the appearance of a librarian rather than a dancer. She certainly wasn't Edward's usual tall slender model type dancer.

"I just needed a little quiet break, that's all," Sydney responded from her folding chair.

"Understandable." Suzanna stubbed out her cigarette and slid into her dance shoes. "Remember, dance session is in fifteen minutes. We'll be doing Tango today." She laughed again and got up to leave. "I've got to get out of this dark hole."

A moment later, the door opened again. Terry Crawford squinted across the room. Mr. Terry, as they called him in the studio, was Sydney's practice partner since they had started dancing at the studio at the same time. He was charming and delightful to talk to but slimy in appearance. Sydney suspected he holed up somewhere on the streets at night. A former actor and male stripper, he could talk like no one else. But his body smell was so offensive that she ended up being his sole dance partner. When they touched hands, she could feel the oiliness of his palms. His greasy hair dipped a few strands over his forehead. He didn't actually take walking steps – he shuffled.

She sat perfectly still and watched as Terry headed over to Suzanna's desk. He reached down and grabbed her purse, took a look inside, then put it back. He had no coat and no dance shoes to change into, so he took no notice of Sydney huddled in the corner. He simply walked out the door and disappeared.

II.

Dance session began at 1:00 each afternoon. The reception desk backed a stone wall that curved elegantly for a few feet into the ballroom. The sound system was tucked into the back of the wall on the side of the dance floor. Suzanna stood at the wall leaning on one of Eddie G.'s famous drums and waited. Teachers tended to straggle in at 1:00. First one would saunter in and then another and another.

Sydney stood along side Antoine and Terry. Big blond Rick Krist swaggered in with Chandler Dane and Anna Smith. Krist was a big burley curly headed man with an engaging smile and a body that didn't say "dancer". His best friend Chandler Dane was exactly the opposite – about 6'4" 125 pounds, he had learned to live by wit rather than brawn.

His round glasses and short cropped hair gave him the look of a little boy on stilts. Anna was a beautiful woman who looked more mature than her eighteen years. She had a round angelic face framed by ringlets of brown curls on top of a round matronly frame. Much to everyone's surprise, she danced with the lightness and grace of a swaying field of colorful flowers.

"Let's get started, ladies and gentlemen," Suzanna Caldwell began. "Take partners for a Tango." Then she put on the pulsing music of Argentina – rhythmic and dramatic.

As the few couples began moving around the floor, the tiny tinkle of the front door once again rang and the loud stamping of feet announced the entry of a few more teachers – late as usual. Megan Meeker poked her head in. "Sorry," she wailed. Her head was wrapped in a colorful scarf, her full lips painted bright red, and her cheeks flushed from the wind. Mimi Clark also poked her head in with a high pitched squeal.

"Hurry, you two," Suzanna instructed sternly. They clomped off down the hall to rid themselves of coats and boots. "Carson will show up in about twenty minutes," Suzanna muttered.

With the group almost complete, Suzanna began her instruction of the Tango. She demonstrated the technique of lowering into the knees, the flares and the cortes. Giggling, half asleep, and boredom written across the faces of her students/teachers, nevertheless, Suzanna continued with her lesson. She knew they would use all the techniques on each lesson today even if it appeared they weren't paying any attention to her instructions. It some how absorbed into their brains and worked out. It was the miracle of education.

With a loud bang, the back door opened. The back door opened to the parking lot directly at the pay booth and was only used by Eddie G. as his downtown condo was right behind the studio. The clatter stopped the class mid dip. They stood still as statues in their poses as Edward Garrett stormed into the ballroom. His long charcoal dress coat flapped around his ankles. His perfectly coiffed curly toupee bounced with each of his long striding steps. He took a moment to pause before the mirror and pat his hair into place without even noticing the stares of the dancers. He scowled and quickly turned back to his pace across the room. "You're late!" he screamed at Carson Hunter who just happened to open the front door at the same time. "No more!" he yelled and grasping the tall thin silver ash tray he threw it across the floor scattering white sand in wispy piles along the hardwood floor. "Clean that up!" he ordered turning on his heels and slamming his office door.

Suzanna stood behind the bongo drum with her fingers pressed tightly across her mouth. Her eyes wide behind her glasses stared contemplating.

"Well, that was smokin'", Chandler Dane cracked. Rick Krist burst into a chuckle and leaned his weight from one foot to the other. Antoine Hawks started for a moment then walked off the floor for a broom and dust pan. Ever the tidy freak, he would do the honors.

"Thanks a lot, Carson," Anna Smith teased. Carson, a man of about thirty years old, stood at 5'6" with dark hair and wire rimmed glasses. His face looked blank as if he wasn't even a part of the whole scene. He wore his uniform – a gray vest and darker gray pants. He shrugged his shoulders and tilted his head slightly to the left as if he was clueless and joined the group in the ballroom.

It was then they noticed the woman. Standing stock still at the front desk was a blond woman of about twenty. She was plain, wearing nondescript pants and blouse with a look of shock on her pale face. All eyes turned to the woman. "I'm Morgan Canfield, the new receptionist," she stammered. "Today is my first day. Is it always like this?"

"You've come at a great time," cracked Chandler. "Usually it's worse. Just kidding," he added hastily.

"He's not kidding," squeaked tiny Mimi Clark. "This is how it is every day." Mimi Clark was a short bottle blond in her mid twenties. She had had a hard life and it showed in her face. She was the only one with a family – a plump daughter of about eight years old and an abusive ex-husband who looked like he was the ring leader of the Hell's Angels.

"I like you," Morgan Canfield said pointing to Mimi. "You tell it like it is. OK, where do I sit and what do I do." Undaunted by the whole situation, Morgan peered around the room and began to circle the desk. "Mine?" she asked. Suzanna nodded as Morgan looking up and down the desk began to make herself at home. "This is my space, and I expect no one to come behind this desk. Understand?" All heads nodded in unison.

Edward Garrett poked his head out of his office. "Meeting!" he yelled.

Milli Mae Carter stomped in through the door. The 4'9" woman in three inch heeled leopard skin boots looked from Morgan to Edward. "What's going on here?" she pulled matching leopard skin gloves off finger by finger.

"You're late," growled Edward. "Get the buffer."

III.

The buffer was used to take the wax off the dance floor. When the floor began to get slippery the teachers grabbed the hunk of paraffin and shaved off small slivers to slow the speed of the floor down. All the wax built up had to eventually be removed. That's when the buffer, that huge monstrosity of a machine came out of the closet — or when Edward Garrett had a point to make, like today.

The teachers stood around the glass topped tables that lined the dance floor waiting to see what was going to happen. The buffer was definitely not a good sign.

Morgan Canfield peeked around the corner from her desk perch and waited expectantly.

"Miss Carter," boomed Edward Garrett. "You're first. Grab the buffer and let's see how you handle this floor." Everyone to Edward was a "Miss" or "Mr.". He hated nicknames and under no circumstances allowed any of his staff to be addressed by their first name.

Milli Mae began to protest. She was a little spitfire of a woman who didn't have any qualms about lodging a complaint. Unfortunately, in this instance it did no good. Finally, she took a deep breath and approached the machine that was about her height and twice as wide. "Plug it in, Antoine. Now give it a go, Miss Carter," Edward instructed.

Antoine put the plug into the socket, and Milli Mae grabbed the handles, flipping on the switch along the side. The buffer immediately began to frantically rotate throwing little Milli Mae to the ground without any effort. Antoine grabbed the machine and flipped off the switch as it groaned to a halt in the middle of the floor.

"Try again, Miss Carter," Edward growled.

"Is this because I was late?" Milli Mae whined as she pulled herself up off the floor. "Because you know it was that bus that was late not me." She brushed off her long tapered skirt and straightened her blouse.

"No, it's not because you were late. Although I won't pay you for this last hour…", Edward stated firmly.

"As if you pay me anyway," Milli Mae quickly mumbled under her breath to which all the other teachers began to snicker.

Edward glared at her then continued. "No, Miss Carter it is not because you were late. It is because you don't know how to handle your students."

Milli Mae glared at him and grabbed the handles. She flipped the switch and again the big buffer began to gyrate. This time Milli Mae hung onto the handles as it lifted her right off the ground and began to twirl uncontrollably. She swung around twice before flying off into the arms of Rick Krist who was laughing hysterically. She never even hit the floor. His massive body held her firmly feet dangling.

"Put me down," Milli Mae ordered. "Yes ma'am," he replied dropping her to her feet.

She again brushed off her skirt. "You want me to go again?" she growled staring at Edward Garrett.

"Let's have Miss Smith give it a go. Let's see how she handles her students." Edward's mouth pressed into smirk and his cheeks puffed out as he gave Anna Smith a daring grin.

Anna was much larger than poor little Milli Mae, but she didn't have the gutsy attitude. She slowly slunk over to the buffer. She tightened her hands in and out of a fist and swayed back and forth between her splayed feet. Her face showed her discontent at the prospect of tackling the flailing buffer. Anna twisted her mouth into a determined pout and slowly placed her hands on the handle. "OK, what do I do here? Just flip this switch here?" As soon as the machine came to life,

Anna Smith flew from one end of the room to the other trailing behind the circling metal menace.

"Control it!" screamed Edward. "That's why you can't teach the Southburys. You have no control." He kept up the banter until she finally flipped the switch to off and defiantly walked off the floor.

"I can too control the Southburys. And that damn buffer has nothing to do with teaching dance lessons," Anna yelled back as she disappeared down the hallway to the teacher's office.

The rest of the teachers stood uncomfortably shifting their weight in the silence of the moment. Edward Garrett walked off the floor to his office. But as he passed the front desk he couldn't help himself. "What are you staring at? Who are you anyway?" he growled at Morgan Canfield as she huddled behind the desk.

"Nothing. And my name is Morgan Canfield," she yelled right back.

"Well, we'll have to change that won't we?" Edward huffed as he slammed the door.

"Great first day," Morgan mumbled as the teachers meandered slowly toward the back office. Antoine of course unplugged the buffer and grabbed the obnoxious piece of equipment to once again banish it to the store room.

"Nice to have you here," Suzanna welcomed with a smile and extended a hand to Morgan. "I'm the supervisor, Suzanna Caldwell."

IV.

The day started officially at three PM. That's when the students began their lessons. Morgan Canfield sat alone at the desk studying the large page of appointments. Each teacher's name was listed at the top of a column. Along the side of the column were the times of day. Appointments were penciled in with a few red and blue pencil markings here and there.

"Sorry I'm late," Joan Ericson apologized as she quickly hung her coat and bustled behind the desk.

"You and everyone else," Morgan commented.

"What?" Joan was in charge of the desk and had hired Morgan a few days ago to take care of the greeting and appointment scheduling. She was a round woman dressed beautifully in a flowing silk skirt, top and matching scarf draped loosely around her neck.

"I met Edward Garrett," Morgan explained.

"Well, that explains everything," Joan grinned showing a set of dimples. Her short brown hair was beginning to gray along the sides. "I started many years ago as a teacher with Mr. Garrett. I admit I had to take a few years off. He was beginning to get on my nerves. But I came back. There's just something about this place that is like none other. It's addicting."

"You can say that again!" Morgan agreed. "They did the buffer in their meeting."

"Oh, dear," Joan sighed. "Don't tell me. Who was the unlucky person?"

"A little midget of a lady..." Morgan tried to carefully choose her words.

"That would be Miss Carter," Joan shook her head.

"Then that pretty larger woman," Morgan continued.

"Miss Smith? Oh, no. I'm sure that didn't go well," Joan let out a puff of air.

"You can say that again," Morgan agreed.

"Well, never mind. Let me show you what needs to be done here. Let me give you a script of how to answer the phone."

Morgan's eyes narrowed. "A script?" she thought. "What have I gotten myself into?"

Joan checked in a few students, and placed a kitchen timer on the top of the desk. "We don't allow clocks here. Too many become clock watchers rather than concentrating on their lessons and students. So we time each lesson hour with this. Lessons are 50 minutes with ten minutes between the start of the next lesson. We begin at five after the hour and end at five to," Joan explained as she checked her own wrist watch for the exact time to begin the timer.

A tall slender couple entered through the door. "May I help you?" Morgan chimed trying to impress Joan with her greeting skills.

"Don't bother with them," Joan chuckled. "He's a teacher here. Richard Gray, meet Morgan Canfield." Joan pointed to his column listed as "Gray". "And this is his lovely wife, Darian."

Richard extended a hand to Morgan. He was very tall with a perfect pale sky blue three piece suit. Morgan didn't think she had ever seen a person with such perfect posture before. He smiled a boyish grin with chin up and nose at an English butler tilt. Then Morgan turned to Darian. Tall and slender as well, Darian was the flip side of Richard. Richard, fair skinned and blond was a stark contrast to the very black

21

haired and tanned Darian. Darian didn't extend her hand to Morgan and stood expressionless to the side of Richard.

"Darian is a flight attendant, so we only see her once in a while," Joan explained trying to give Darian a smile. Darian remained stone faced. The two Grays said their goodbyes quickly, and Darian left.

Richard leaned over to check his schedule. "No one is allowed back behind this desk," Joan continued her training procedure. "They will try to pull one past you and sneak behind, but it's not allowed."

Morgan smiled in anticipation of her first reprimand to a teacher who tried to defy that rule. She would enjoy this power.

"Let's see," Joan scanned the sheet, "are we missing any of the other teachers? Monroe, Terry, Hawks, Caldwell, Meeker, Clark, Krist, Dane, Smith, Gray, Hunter, Carter, Fritz. Oh, yes. Mr. Fritz only comes in at night. So you haven't met him yet. Don't take anything from him. He's been here for years. You'd think he'd take his job a little more seriously. He's here for the ladies. That's about it. Watch him carefully." She pointed to the sign that hung prominently behind the desk in big bold letters – "No Student Teacher Fraternization."

Morgan studied the sign and smiled. "I'd be glad to enforce that one," she said firmly. The music blared in the background. A current disco song pounded the stone wall behind the desk. "Can I wear earplugs?"

V.

The end of the day on Thursday was a dance party. The social dances were held Thursday nights and the disco parties on Fridays. Everyone was expected to attend. The lights turned low, the students seated at the glass topped tables and standing along the side waited in anticipation for the music to begin. The teachers mingled and chatted with middle aged to older adults.

Sydney Monroe enjoyed these parties but felt a little intimidated. Although she was a trained ballet and jazz dancer, this ballroom stuff was still somewhat of a mystery. It seemed to her that the students knew more than she did. But she put another layer of lipstick on, took a mint from the dish at the front desk, and moved out to the ballroom to mingle along with the rest. She still didn't have the schedule down and tried to look around at the others to see what was expected.

First, a Fox Trot began to play. Edward Garrett had slipped behind his side by side bongo drums in front of the sound system. He was the DJ tonight as usual. The pound of the music seemed to spark his energy. He was a night person anyway, so nine o'clock was his time to really move. The next song was a Cha Cha, and he began to pound on the drums much to the annoyance of many of the older students.

One of the students Sydney was dancing with began to mutter. "Doesn't he ever stop? Can't you get him to go out of town so we can get some decent music and less drums?"

"He doesn't listen to me I'm afraid," Sydney sighed.

"Well, he should!" came the frustrated reply. Sydney smiled.

Each party required the talents of the teaching staff not only to dance each dance with the students, but to have one couple perform a show routine. The list of assigned dances and couplings was posted each month in the teacher's office. Tonight Mimi Clark was performing with Antoine Hawks. Antoine was the head of the new student department, and Mimi was one of the teachers he supervised. She let out a little squeal as they took the floor. Their assigned dance was the Rumba, a slow Latin dance with a rhythmic beat to the music. Mimi gave her partner a goofy smile that set the audience laughing then danced a beautiful romantic show number. Sydney could tell that she was a ballet dancer as well. Her fluid arm motion and flexible body positions showed well trained skills. The two of them received a thunderous applause.

"Now let's all find a partner for a Rumba," Edward announced over the PA system. The group crowded the floor for a dance to the same music. As the dance ended, Edward further announced, "All teachers please report to the teacher's office for an important meeting." Sydney knew Edward did this after every party to get the crowds out and not lingering in the reception area. She headed back to the office to wait. Her bus would be coming in about twenty minutes, so she hoped everyone would leave quickly.

When the teachers finally all gathered in the back room, Edward actually entered the dark and smoky room himself. "Meeting for real," he announced.

"Mr. Garrett," Sydney raised her hand frantically. "I really need to leave. My bus will be here any minute."

Edward Garrett sputtered noisily. "Well...OK. But be prepared for meetings at a moments notice from now on."

The next morning, Sydney didn't go in to exercise. She had errands to run before getting to the studio. Standing at the mirror in the ballroom, Terry Crawford joined her. "You missed a dinger of meeting, that's for sure," he began.

"Oh, yeah. What did I miss? I didn't think anything could top the buffer," Sydney laughed as she practiced a fifth position in Merengue.

"Eddie G. asked me what you thought of him," Terry eyed her with a gleam.

Sydney stopped. "What does that mean? And what exactly did you tell him?"

"I told him you thought he was a little Hitler," Terry smirked.

"Oh, no. You didn't?" Sydney gasped.

"Don't you remember referring to him that way just last week?" Terry reminded her.

"But that was only for you to hear. Not him!" Sydney seethed. Didn't the guy know any better than to keep something like that to himself? "What did he say then?"

"Not much." Terry got into dance position and began to practice the step with her. Sydney glared into his face. It didn't seem to bother him at all. He just kept smiling at her. His palms felt greasy and his sport coat smelled of sweat. She wanted so badly to tell him – to hurt him back, but she kept her tongue.

Suzanna entered the ballroom and announced, "Dance session."

The teachers lined up in front of the mirror to practice arm and feet positions. Suzanna was next to Sydney positioning Rick Krist's arms. Her arms extended, Sydney's mind began to wander until a hoarse voice whispered in her ear. "Little Hitler, huh?"

She glanced up to see Edward Garrett's curly hair bobbing behind her in the mirror. Contrary to what she had expected, he wasn't angry. In fact, his mouth was curled into a cheerful smile. She closed her eyes and shuddered.

"I didn't actually say…" she began.

"And no more missing of morning exercise, understand?" Edward whispered.

"I was just tired …" Sydney tried to explain.

He cut her off with a laugh and continued on to his office to remove his long wool coat. "What was his game?" she wondered. She felt like a mouse being played with by the big nasty cat – kept alive for entertainment purposes. Inside she detested Terry Crawford. Why had he done that to her?

After dance session and meeting, Terry came up to her. "I kind of feel bad for getting you into trouble. Care to go to lunch? My treat." Terry's eyes darted around the room as if he didn't want anyone else to hear him. She suspected treating someone to lunch wasn't exactly in his budget.

"McDonalds?" she suggested. It was across the street, and she thought probably one of Terry's favorites judging by the burger and onion smell he always came in with.

"Great!" he sort of leered strangely.

When they got to the counter, Sydney ordered her favorite Quarter Pounder with cheese. Terry pulled out a fifty dollar bill, and Sydney did a double take. She wanted to ask him where he got that. Getting paid at the studio she knew was a problem.

Terry ranted on about strange things during lunch and then when they went to throw out their trash, he actually dropped the whole tray into the trash rather than just the paper products. "Oops!" he giggled but just kept walking out the door.

When they got back to the studio, the dance floor was almost empty. An elderly woman was screaming at Edward Garrett in the reception area. "I think it's disgusting," she was saying. "You drive that brand new black Mercedes and can't even pay your teachers."

Edward sputtered. "And where did you hear that? Who is your teacher?"

"Never you mind where I heard that," she stood right in front of him glaring into his face. "I know it's true. You've done it before. I've been in this studio for many, many years Mr. Garrett, and I don't miss much. All the money I pay for my lessons and you go and spend it on luxuries for yourself. Disgusting. If I didn't like my teachers so much, I'd leave and take my business elsewhere."

Evidently she did spend a lot of money at the studio or Edward would have told her to do just that. Instead, he took a deep breath, put on a huge smile and said, "Now, Mrs. Lang, I know we can resolve this matter. I'm sure what you heard is false. But to reassure you, I would love to give you a free lesson."

Mrs. Lang shuddered at his reply and turned abruptly leaving.

Before anyone could react further, there came a scream from the teacher's office. Sydney, Edward, Morgan, and Terry ran down the hall to the half opened door. Was someone hurt? Was it a mouse?

Mimi Clark stood in the middle of the floor holding her large over the shoulder throw purse. "It's gone!"

"Now calm down Miss Clark," Edward Garrett put his hands up to stop her loud screaming voice. Megan Meeker stood behind her mouth gaping. "What's gone?" Edward continued.

"My money, that's what! I had two fifty dollar bills in my purse and one of them is missing!"

Sydney turned quickly to catch Terry's eye, but he was no where to be found. Her mind wandered as she briefly heard Edward trying to get the full story from Mimi. Mimi was not crying but angry – very angry. Edward was asking why she would keep so much money in her purse and why such large bills but Sydney didn't listen to the answer. Her mind was wandering back to the time she caught Terry going through Suzanna's purse. Was it a coincidence? What about his fifty dollar bill at lunch today? Should she say something?

Quickly she left the room and went to find Suzanna Caldwell. She was a person who she could trust with this information as well as a person who would know what to do about it.

VI.

Saturday. A day to sleep in for sure. But Sydney had missed exercise class the day before, and Edward Garrett's warning played havoc with her mind. She got into a leotard, tights with lots of runs, a sweatshirt and pants. Grabbing her raincoat she just made the bus and got to the studio a few moments early as usual. The door was locked but the lights were on. She banged on the door and waited. Nothing. Edward must be in his office and not able to hear her.

Amanda arrived in her floor length fur. "Not hearing you out here, huh?" she said peering in through the door as she fished her keys from her pocket. "Well, we'll just change that." Amanda's lips curled a little at the ends.

Sydney turned right to hang up her coat, and Amanda turned left to go into Edward's office.

Sydney heard the gasp. It wasn't a scream, but more of a surprised intake of air. Amanda was standing at Edward's doorway as Sydney rushed up behind her to peer over her shoulder. Edward Garrett was lying face down on his desk. A pool of blood covered the desk beneath his crumpled head and shoulders.

31

VII.

The body had been photographed and removed in a body bag. The office was decorated with the bright yellow streamers that indicated no one was to enter, and the police detective was interviewing Joan Ericson. Amanda sat silently on the couch in the reception area. Antoine Hawks had his arm around her shoulders and was patting her hand. Sydney was sitting on the window sill next to the coat rack watching and listening to the silence and the spattered conversations.

"The question isn't who was Edward Garrett's enemy, but rather who wasn't. Edward was a man who everyone found easy to hate," Joan Ericson was telling the detective.

Only a few of the teachers had been called immediately about Edward's death. Suzanna, of course was here. Antoine and Joan. The rest would be in shortly for interviews to see if anyone had observed anything last evening. Edward had been killed during the night after the studio had officially closed. The weapon had been a small caliber pistol – one easily concealed but definitely indicating a premeditated act rather than an accident. The killer didn't need a key to get in or out. Eddie G. could have let someone else in and then after the shooting, that person had simply left the lights on and walked out the door with it locking behind. Then again, the person could have just stayed behind after everyone else left. There were enough places in the studio to hide. The glass windows in the parking lot entry made it hard to shoot someone out on the dance floor or in the reception area. Someone might have walked by at that time. But Edward's office. It was concealed from view. A gun shot in a parking ramp would likely appear to be from a car backfiring. No one would call police. And no one had.

The finger print team has white powder all over the reception area, but whose prints weren't on the door? With all the students, it would be impossible to find a print that didn't belong.

Sydney observed. Amanda Garrett, the grieving widow, was calm. She seemed to show no emotion other than shock at seeing a dead body. With the rumors that Amanda and Edward were headed for divorce, there may be motive there, Sydney surmised. Edward had a dalliance for other women despite having a locally famous and beautiful wife. The two came into class separately and from different directions indicating that they no longer came from the same place. That was something to think about, Sydney thought.

Edward had definitely irritated Anna Smith and Milli Mae Carter with the buffer incident. They were both angry and humiliated by

Edward's little stunt. Morgan Canfield had gotten an ear and eyeful in her first week of work. Carson Hunter had been the brunt of the ashtray throwing incident. Even she herself had an embarrassing "Little Hitler" incident. Of course, some of that had been due to good old Terry. Terry, he was a strange one as well. This whole week had shown a side of Terry that was unsettling. Joan and Suzanna had both had their share of ups and downs with Edward. They had years of strange and interesting situations they could undoubtedly recount that would give them negative feelings for Edward. Sydney knew that she would have to dig only a little bit to find out more about Edward's history. And who was the one who had told Mrs. Lang about the bouncing of the paychecks? Craig Fritz and Carson Hunter both taught her dance lessons. It could have been someone else entirely. Mrs. Lang seemed to know about everything that went on in this studio. She would have stories to tell. Even she had motive if she thought Edward was taking her money fraudulently. This would be a hard case, for sure.

Each teacher was ushered into a small private studio about the size of a closet only with hard wood floors and mirrored walls. The door would close for a few minutes. Then the next one would replace that teacher. Sydney would be one of the last to be interviewed as she was actually on the scene when the body was discovered.

One by one the teachers were interviewed and then told they could leave. "Miriam Southerland", the voice called into the reception area.

Sydney squinted. Who was Miriam Southerland? Mimi Clark noisily rose and squawked an acknowledgement.

Megan Meeker smirked. She could see Sydney's confusion about the name. "That's Mimi's real name," she whispered. "Miriam is her given first name, and Southerland her married name. She goes by her maiden name here. It is kind of a protection thing as well as more comfortable for her." Sydney nodded an understanding.

When it was finally time for Sydney's interview she shuffled into the small area to the chair set up in the temporary interview space. The questions seemed generic. Why was she there on a Saturday morning? What had she observed when the body was discovered? Had she noticed anything unusual last night? Did she know of anyone with a motive? That question was tougher. She was glad that Joan Ericson had already brought up the possibility that there were many with motive. So

Sydney's observations seemed to fit right in with that earlier statement. She recalled all the incidents that had occurred that week.

VII.

Monday was quiet. Everyone seemed to be in a solemn mood. In dance session, Sydney was partnered with Terry. They tried to work on Swing.

"What's the matter," Terry leaned in close with a big sarcastic grin. "Can't you turn anymore, or what?"

"If you would lead a turn, I would do a turn," Sydney replied tersely. With that, Terry cranked her arm and scowled at her. "Ouch. That wasn't a lead. Why don't you go dance with someone else if you're going to dance like that," Sydney stood back with her arms folded across her chest. With that Terry stalked off and grabbed Megan Meeker's arm.

"Let's dance," he demanded.

"Let go of me." She wriggled free from his grasp and stood back flicking her hands. "You smell. And you're greasy. Don't you ever shower or bathe?" Megan's nose began to wrinkle up. Terry wore a pale blue suit that had once belonged to Edward Garrett. Edward bought only the finest when he shopped, so the suit had been a beautiful Italian

36

garment that he had grown tired of wearing. He had brought it in with several others to sell to the staff at a reduced price. He always demanded his staff look well put together, and you can be sure his intention was to get Mr. Kelly to dress better. Even with the nice suit, Kelly looked sloppy. The suit was wrinkled and looked slept in. The pants hung down too long so the cuffs dragged under his shoes. He swept his hand through his slicked back hair and tightened his face into a bitter stare.

"Mr. Terry," Suzanna Caldwell addressed him from the other side of the room. "Why don't you go to the bathroom and clean up a bit?" He turned abruptly and glared at her. Without another word, he walked away.

The rest of the group began to dance. The energy level was low and the music played softly in the background. No one spoke for the rest of the session.

Megan Meeker walked over to the glass topped table after dance session and retrieved her hat. Megan was noted for her hats. The short cut bright red hair was always adorned with a scarf wrap or a decorative hat. Today she wore a silk dress of bright red cinched at the waist with a tight leather belt and a straw brimmed hat with red ribbons and bright cherries. Her full lips were bright red to match.

The rest of the staff milled around the tables, not ready to sit for the meeting just yet. Suddenly a commotion ripped through the studio. There was a loud thud and then muffled yells coming from the hallway.

In the hallway Rick Krist was holding Terry against the wall banging his head loudly. Rick was a big burley guy, and he nearly took up the width of the hallway. He was angry and yelling right in Terry's face.

Terry was pressed against the wall with a frightened look on his face as Rick pressed his forearm into his throat. "Don't you ever do that again, you little pervert," Rick was screaming in a low but forceful voice.

"Rick!" Suzanna gasped from behind him. "Let go of him right now. We've already had enough around here with Mr. Garrett's murder and all. Let him go, please." Suzanna was pressing her fingers into her mouth so her pleading was soft and breathy.

Rick let up a little and finally with one last slam to the head of Terry, backed away. Terry held his throat but suddenly a huge sarcastic look of triumph spread across his face. He stared defiantly at Rick causing Rick to make a quick start for him again. But by that time Terry had slid down the wall and was heading for the back room.

Rick turned to the gathering group of teachers huddled in the narrow hallway. "The little slime bag left his crab cream in the men's bathroom. I mean, come on. There's a limit to what we should have to take," Rick's mustache curled up on the left side and he shook his head in disgust.

"That is disgusting," Antoine agreed. Antoine always looked perfect. Perfect hair, perfect teeth, perfect suit with a perfect vest and perfect silk tie. He straightened his perfect pearly white shirt and shuddered as he trailed back to the ballroom.

Morgan sat at the front desk shaking her head. "What have I gotten myself into? First the buffer, then the murder, and now the crab cream. I could easily be driven to murder someone myself." Sydney couldn't help but chuckle at Morgan's synopsis of the situation. She had made a tense situation somehow humorous. Morgan looked around to see a person seated on the couch and quickly added with a stammer, "Oops! I mean if I hadn't only worked here for a day or two and didn't even know the man."

Sitting in the reception area was the police detective here to conduct a few more interviews. Had he been here during the Krist/Terry incident? If not, he was sure to hear about it. Had he watched Sydney

39

rebuff Terry's dance moves? He was sure to hear about that as well. The man just sort of blended into the wall. He was nondescript in appearance and clothing. He could very well have been here through the whole thing and no one would have noticed. Sydney frowned. What would he think? Should she mention the purse incident? Who knows how long money had been taken from purses in the back room. If Terry had been taking small amounts of money, no one would notice. They would just think they had somehow miscalculated what they had in their purse. But the fifty dollar bill was too big to miss. That may have been his big mistake.

Suzanna stood up trying to get everyone's attention. The whole staff except for Craig Fritz was whispering noisily around the glass tables waiting for the meeting to begin. Terry Crawford sat behind everyone else at a lone table in the corner.

"Listen," Suzanna finally said firmly. "We have obligations that continue even with the death of Mr. Garrett. We have a show to do tonight at Frankie's. And that show is still on."

Frankie's was a popular disco down the street from the studio. The staff usually led by Eddie G. and Amanda did one evening show a week and one happy hour show on Fridays. The club usually requested the complex rope hustle routine that Eddie G. had choreographed to a song from a currently playing movie about the disco scene. The audience loved it.

"We're going to have to regroup and practice sometime today between lessons. Do you all have some free time this afternoon?" Suzanna continued.

"I have lessons all afternoon," Anna Smith moaned. She loved doing shows although Eddie G. always chided her about her weight.

"OK, then we'll form a team of four couples. Sydney you dance with Richard, Antoine with Mimi, Megan with Rick and Milli with Terry."

Milli groaned. "Terry doesn't know the rope hustle well enough to dance the routine," Milli whined.

"Terry do you know it or not?" Suzanna shot the question to the back corner.

"I'm busy tonight, anyway," Terry shot back loudly with a crooked smirk on his face.

"Fine. Milli you dance with Rick, and Megan you call Craig Fritz. Get him in here to practice. He can do it. You can follow his lead, and you're more his size." Craig was tall and skinny and had been

41

around for years. Unfortunately he wasn't very dependable. He would come in though. Craig loved to do shows. Anything for an audience and a few claps.

Megan grumbled something no one understood but nodded. "Practice at 4:00," she announced to the group. "I can get Craig out of bed by 4. Can I go call him right now?" she asked.

"You'd better," Suzanna sighed. "You'll have to wear the black, red and blue disco costumes." Another groan from the group. The disco costumes were Edward's idea. A slinky leo with crisscrosses here and there that covered hardly anything topped with a long slit skirt. The skirts always managed to trip up whoever was forced to wear them. Two of the skirts slit up the sides with the center sewn together. If you lifted your foot at all, you were sure to catch a heel in the sewn section. It was inevitable.

Sydney could see Suzanna losing her composure. She wasn't one who really wanted to take charge of these things now that Edward was gone. Suzanna's usual calm demeanor was agitated and troubled as she began to realize all that she would be organizing.

"We'll see about the Friday show after we get through this one," Suzanna added and then let the group get ready for their teaching day and their performance that evening.

Sydney gravitated toward Richard Gray and begged his time for a quick rehearsal before Craig rounded out the group. Richard was so very perfect or was it uptight? Always dressed in a three piece suit in a pale pastel color that looked great with his fair hair and coloring, Richard rarely showed his playful side. He only occasionally let his guard down, and on those rare instances he was great. He would throw his partner into a ride like maneuver that brought laughter to the point of tears to all who watched. Sydney hoped he would be in one of these moods today. She could use a fun filled rehearsal after this weekend's event.

"I gotta quick call my wife and let her know I'll be doing the show. Be right back," Richard disappeared but seemed upbeat.

The rope hustle was an energetic number that required lots of big straight arm movements and down to the floor dips that were almost impossible to get up from, but Sydney loved to do this dance with Richard. He was always great at supporting his partner and making it really easy even for the most difficult steps. The rehearsal went well. They arranged the couples two in front and two in the back off set so the

43

whole group could be seen from the front. The floor at Frankie's was surrounded on three sides by tables and people who would press right up to the edge of the floor to get a good look. They would do OK tonight in spite of everything. The pounding music and flashing lights would put everyone in a performance mood.

VIII.

Sydney pulled on the bright blue costume and refreshed her make-up. It didn't matter if Eddie G. was around or not. Everyone knew what was expected when doing a show. The make-up was heavier for visibility under the stage lights. She darkened her liner and eye shadow. Then she coated her lips with a bright red shade. Hollowing her cheeks, she applied a new layer of blush then pulled the top of her permed bob into a disco tail that flopped to the side like a drippy faucet. Perfect.

The makeup and the costumes had been a stretch for her at first. As a child she had studied ballet and jazz. She had first walked into the studio dressed in a red plaid flannel shirt and jeans with no makeup and her hair pulled back into a pony tail. Edward had quickly reprimanded her. "We look professional in this studio – dresses are mandatory and makeup should be applied before ever walking out on this dance floor," he had said abruptly. "Heels are required dance shoes," he had continued. "Tomorrow you will look presentable." And she had. At first she had only one dress that she laundered every evening to wear the next day, and Antoine had to show her how to apply mascara. It had been a process, but now she understood the importance of presentation. Now she was going out to perform for crowds of people who expected not only to see a great dance performance but also a dancer who looked like a performer. She could do that.

She slid into her rain coat that covered the hideous costume and left with the rest of the group for the block and a half walk to "Frankie's". The night was comfortable. The darkness of the sky contrasted with the lights of the downtown skyscrapers. Neon signs and streetlights glimmered against the black sky. Small groups of people walked past in an array of unique attire. Heads turned occasionally when a particularly unusual outfit passed. That was the charm of the city. No one even noticed the slinky bright costumes of the group from the studio.

Frankie's was an art deco building nestled between two modern office buildings. The stone front was beautiful with unique crevices and niches – the inside loud and pulsing. They were waived through the cover charge check post. Inside the small floor glistened under the strobed disco ball that flashed rays of light around the room. The tables weren't yet filled, but would be soon. The show always brought wannabe dancers to view the tightly choreographed moves and leggy dancers in slightly revealing costumes.

Richard spotted his wife Darian back in one of the corners and excused himself to talk with her briefly before the group headed back to the dressing room behind the stage. Darian was a beauty. She was tall, but not model tall and slender with glistening black hair. The two of them were like salt and pepper, night and day, good and evil. Richard with his blond hair and fair complexion was in stark contrast to Darian's dark sultriness. She rarely smiled but always looked elegant. Tonight she wore a black suit with a bit of a camisole peeking through the opening of the tailored jacket. Darian always wore black – Richard always pastel or cream. They stood together erect and formal without exchanging a hug or kiss like many couples would. Then Richard joined the group again, and they all retreated to the dressing room to get rid of coats and prepare for the show.

Sydney stretched her legs and took in deep breathes of air. She rotated her shoulders and flexed her arms. Then she slid into her dance shoes – a pair of three inch heeled opened toed Latin shoes in a gold lame finish.

Craig Fritz joined the group – late as usual. He had on an opened collar white shirt with full sleeves and tight black flared pants. Frankie's was one of his favorite hangouts so he had probably stopped at each table along the way to greet friends and enemies. He was a good dancer and one who was always out at the clubs showing off his talents. That made him very popular with the ladies and unpopular with their boyfriends. He was definitely in the dancing game for the recognition and fame. That was why his appearance at the studio was infrequent. He and Eddie G. had a relationship of mutual respect for their dance prowess and pick up lines, but each felt they had more class than the other. So there was always an air of standoff rivalry.

Could Craig have shot Edward? Sydney looked at Craig's slim dark brown mustache and slightly mopped head of hair. Yes, there was just enough friction between them to cause tension. Craig was a man without scruples. He would do anything that benefited Craig Fritz. That was just the way he was. Most accepted that and ignored it as long as it didn't affect them. He kept his distance from trouble whenever possible.

Megan, Mimi and Antoine giggled in the corner but kept an eye out toward the floor for the signal the show was to begin. Rick Krist leaned against the wall with his eyes closed. This would be one of his first shows now that Edward wasn't there as the fourth man. He was pondering something – probably the sequence of the routine. Not someone to get nervous, he seemed calm and collected when they nudged him to head out to the floor. His passive demeanor was in stark contrast to his volatile mood toward Terry earlier that day.

Sydney and Richard were one of the front couples. She knew they would look good. Richard was always precise with his movements and excellent in his leads. They would look great. The music began to pound and the crowd began to gather as they quickly found their spots on the floor and waited for the cue in the music to begin. She could feel her body bounce with the tempo and her muscles tense for the first beat of the routine. Then it began, and they were off. Only a little under two minutes, yet an eternity when dancing. Sydney knew she was doing the movements, but couldn't actually focus in on doing anything. It was like an out of body experience when performing. It was if you weren't actually there, but watching from somewhere in the back of the room.

The people in the crowd were closing in on the stage – all standing to get a better look, but the dancers seemed unaware of their presence due to the bright spot lights that glared in their eyes. They could feel the breathing and the cheers. The music ended and the clapping followed them off the stage to the dressing room.

Craig Fritz was out the door and ready to mingle as soon as the routine was over. He would find someone to take home that night but only after dancing with all the lovely wide eyed beauties that clustered near the floor to watch him move and show off. Richard paused as if not quite ready to join his wife. Rick Krist showed signs of relief. His shoulders relaxed and his face reflected a sloppy grin. He would go out to the club floor to collect his praise in a moment. For now, he would stand in the corner and let the tension evaporate like the sweat that glistened his brow.

Sydney grabbed her rain coat. She could just about make the next bus home if she hurried. Richard gave her a proper "Thank you for the dance." They walked together across the crowded room dodging the people. Groups clustered around tables and in corners holding colorful drinks decorated with umbrellas and cherries. Craig was coaxing Darian out to the floor. She had that same cold stare on her face but was

49

listening intently to his banter as he led her to the center of the room. She glanced at Richard and gave him a quick sharp glare then returned to the cold stare. If Sydney hadn't been watching her so closely it would have been likely that she would have missed it altogether. But it was definitely a split second of change that bothered Sydney. Was Darian upset that Sydney was walking with Richard? Was she jealous? Or was she angry with Craig for dragging her into an uncomfortable situation on the dance floor? It was hard to determine. Sydney paused. She could take a moment to watch. Her curiosity got the better of her.

Darian was smooth and very comfortable dancing with Craig. It was true that Craig could lead anyone and make them look fabulous. It was his gift. But it was more than that. Darian was confident and not in the least bit intimidated by Craig's spins and flash. She danced right along with everything he led and did so with grace and flare.

"I didn't know Darian was such a wonderful dancer," Sydney commented. Richard stood and watched as well. "Yeah," he grinned a bit. "She's a good dancer." His feelings were just as secret as Darian's. Sydney didn't know if he was proud or just being sarcastic.

Craig kept Darian out on the floor for another dance. She didn't seem to mind. Her attentions weren't on Craig at all. She seemed to be staring out into space somewhere other than Frankie's dance floor. Rick Krist was out dancing with Megan, and Mimi was dragging some poor spectacled businessman out on the floor as he dug his heels in to protest. She was too determined to take no for an answer. Then Sydney spotted Terry standing against the back wall. His face began to twist in rage as he watched the dancers laughing and twirling on the floor.

"I thought Terry was too busy to do the show tonight," Sydney motioned to the back wall. Richard just shrugged and ignored her comment. When Sydney looked back, Terry was gone. She glanced through the crowd but couldn't spot the greasy gloss of black hair nor the pale blue suit anywhere.

Chandler Dane joined them. About six foot four and a hundred twenty five pounds, Chandler was a bean pole with the comic sense of a stand up comedian. He could always come up with a quick answer to any comment. He was dressed nicely in a lavender silk shirt and pleated dark gray pants. He was so tall and slender that when Milli Mae Carter came up behind him, she seemed about as tall as his legs were long. She gave him a wack to the arm and completely upset his drink. "Come on," she ordered and grabbed his hand. Despite Chandler's lack of teaching experience, he was a great dancer. Frankie's was one of his favorite spots, and everyone knew him. They would call out his name or nod an acknowledgement as he passed by to get to the floor. His wire rimmed glasses slid down a notch on his nose as he led Milli Mae through a quick Cha Cha. She shrieked with excitement as he spun her around the floor. Sydney had to leave quickly to catch that bus.

IX.

"We're continuing the morning dance sessions," Amanda Garrett had mentioned the day before as she slid on her fur coat to leave. Sydney knew that was a direct hint to get herself in for the morning stretch. She had gotten home early after the show, so the alarm clock didn't give her too much of a start in the morning.

Amanda would probably get the studio. It was beneficial for her to keep everything going as usual so as not to break the routine. The staff would stay. There was no question of that. No one was too fond of Edward or his moody tirades. It was the dance that kept everyone there in spite of the problems with the pay checks. They were all dance addicts. She smiled at that thought. Yes, she was a dance addict.

Amanda was already there when Sydney arrived. The office was still taped off, so Amanda's coat and clothes were piled on the sofa in the

52

lobby. The music was playing a sad, sentimental melody, and Amanda was slowly stretching. The song must bring back special memories. Amanda was not paying attention to Sydney's arrival. She was lost in her own space and time.

Sydney sat down in the middle of the floor and began to stretch. "Oh, hello there," Amanda snapped out of her mood as soon as the song stopped and moved to a faster beat selection. "I hope it's not just the two of us. Not that I mind just you and me, but I really need some people around me right now. It feels better," Amanda hesitated to explain.

Antoine clamored in the front door making the bell ring loudly. His voice shouted a greeting as he stomped his feet and tramped to the back room to change. He gave Amanda a long hug when he returned to the dance floor. Amanda pressed her head into his shoulder and her body began to shake slightly.

"That's OK, honey," Antoine soothed as he held her close. "Let it all out." But when Amanda stepped away, her eyes were dry and clear. She gave Antoine a Mona Lisa smile, held his hand for a lingering moment, then pulled away to begin her exercises again. The morning session was quiet. Very calm and quiet.

Quiet that is until the door flew open. Terry Crawford was loudly shouting at someone who followed his closely.

"Get away from me," Terry shouted.

"We need to talk with you further Mr. Crawford," the person behind him said calmly. Sydney recognized the man as one of the police detectives who had conducted the interviews. Another man was following the detective. Both men took hold of Terry's arms and prevented him from going into the hallway toward the back teachers' office. Terry was mumbling a protest, but to no avail.

"We have some finger prints we need to discuss with you," the first detective was trying to explain. "And some photos that need further explanation."

"Everyone's finger prints are in that room. It's not like I'm the only one," Terry's voice began to bellow. "Those pictures are old. They have nothing to do with this situation. Nothing at all." Terry's acting voice began to waiver a bit.

They led Terry out of the studio just as Joan Ericson came in. She stopped to take in the scene then hung up her coat tucking her leather gloves into the pockets. She carried a large briefcase that she slid behind the reception desk and began to busy herself.

"What was that about?" Antoine Hawks slid around the corner. "What do they have to ask Terry about?"

"They found his prints on the top of Edward's desk. There are a few sets of prints that one might expect to be there, but Terry isn't someone who usually was invited into Edward's little den, now was he? They want to find out why those prints are there along with some very explicit photos of Terry. I guess he was a stripper or something. The police called me this morning and asked that I meet them here in case they had any trouble getting Terry to cooperate."

Joan wasn't exactly Terry's favorite person, so it seemed a bit odd that she was the one called in for this mission. However, considering the other people they might have called, Joan would be a logical choice. She had insight into most things that went on around the studio.

Milli Mae Carter stormed into the reception area. "Hey, what's going on? Why are they walking Terry out to the police car?"

"Just another interview," Joan explained calmly. "They have a few more questions for him, that's all."

"Well, has anyone seen Chandler yet today?" Milli Mae quickly changed the subject. "We're rehearsing for our routine tonight at the party." Her face suddenly became deviously comical. A tiny woman under five feet tall, Milli Mae was what one could consider "cute". And she would always be "cute" no matter how she aged. It was just her, that's all. "Wait until you see what we're doing," she giggled and pranced back to the teacher's office to wait.

X.

The weekly parties were always fun. The students came to dance, watch routines by the staff, and let loose a little with their dancing. Starting at nine o'clock, it lasted for two hours giving everyone a chance to warm up for an evening out at Frankie's or one of the other clubs in the area.

As the clock neared ten thirty, the crowd began to ready for the staff show that would entertain this week. There was a list posted in the teachers' office assigning one female teacher to one male teacher for that week's show. It also assigned a dance to be performed so the variety could be demonstrated to those who weren't familiar with all of the dance styles. Tonight Milli Mae Carter was paired with Chandler Dane for a Fox Trot/Swing combination. Although the Fox Trot was considered a slower dance, it could be done to the same music as a Swing if the song were appropriate.

Milli Mae and Chandler had changed clothes in the kitchen area behind the dance floor so no one could see them prior to the routine. Milli Mae walked out in a blue dress and white pinafore. Her short cut hair was pulled into two tiny pigtails. The crowd snickered. But when tall, lean Chandler walked out in a scarecrow outfit the crowd positively exploded. He had straw sticking out from his shirt and pants. The ankles and wrists were tied with pieces of twine, and his face was painted with a chalky white substance. A large floppy hat hid his short cropped hair. They danced to a song from the movie "The Wiz". The music was fun and lively, but their height difference and great costumes made the number even more humorous. The crowd clapped and cheered in delight.

When the number was over, Suzanna Caldwell announced the last dance of the evening. Now that Edward was dead, Suzanna had taken over as the MC for the night. She stood behind the tall tom-tom drums that Edward usually beat on throughout the party. Tonight they were silent, and Suzanna stood in quiet respect the entire evening. People didn't quite know how to react – serious or lighthearted. The evening had been rather serious until the dance routine. Now the mood was broken, and everyone took on a few minutes of lightness. People actually left laughing.

When the crowd had dispersed, the staff was left. "Hey, can I catch a ride home?" Milli Mae asked grabbing Chandler's arm. She had shed the Dorothy dress and pigtails. Chandler on the other hand still remained in his scarecrow getup. The makeup and straw were not easily removed, so he just kept everything intact.

"Sure," he grinned. Chandler drove an old beat up C hevy with rusty doors. Milli Mae didn't drive like many of the teachers. Some didn't because they simply couldn't afford a vehicle. Others like Milli Mae hadn't bothered to get their license. Living in the city, the bus was always available for transportation. Milli Mae lived in a rather seedy area of town, and whenever she could get a ride rather than take the bus, she jumped at the chance to avoid the late night street hustlers and gang bangers.

The night didn't end in the best circumstances as Milli Mae would relate the next morning when everyone was in for dance session. She bustled in late and demanded to know if Chandler was in yet. The rest of the staff began to circle curiously. "No, Chandler's not in yet," Suzanna answered with a hint of surprise. "Why?"

"You would not believe what happened last night," Milli Mae breathlessly related. "Chandler was driving me home, and we had just gotten past that bar on the corner of Lexington."

"That hole in the wall?" Antoine asked.

"Exactly. That one on the corner that looks like it's abandoned. You know my neighborhood isn't that great, but all the locals hang out there. So there was a crowd that was gathered in front. Just before we got to the corner, some drunk guy steps out right into our path. We didn't even see him coming. He must have been slumped down behind a parked car. Well, we didn't see him, and we hit him," Milli Mae became animated and faster in her speech.

"What?" the rest of the staff reacted in shock and surprise. "What happened?"

"We weren't going that fast, but he kind of flew over the hood. He was so drunk that it didn't even seem to phase him. He kind of got up and stumbled away. We started to stop and get out of the car to see how he was, but then the group of his friends from the corner saw what had happened and began to come toward us. We jumped back into the car and tried to drive away. Chandler was in that stupid scarecrow getup. They started shouting and bouncing the car. You know that car isn't much anyway. But we finally gunned the engine and drove away. They were all yelling and running after us for about a block or so. It was really scary. When we got to my house, Chandler called the police to report it. I don't know what happened after that. He kind of disappeared with the cops. So is he here?" Milli Mae demanded.

The group just looked at her in disbelief. "That was quite a story," Suzanna paused. The others nodded and began to whisper among themselves. "No, we haven't seen him yet," Suzanna answered. "Maybe we had better try to call him and see what happened." She looked at Morgan sitting at the desk shaking her head.

"I'm on it," Morgan replied and thumbed through her rolodex. "This place is something else," she was mumbling under her breath. "Hit a drunk. Chased by an angry mob. Too much."

Just as Morgan began to lift the receiver, Chandler Dane opened the front door. He looked tired. No longer dressed in the scarecrow straw, he seemed pale and quiet.

Milli Mae ran over to him and took a leap into his arms.

"What happened to you? Why didn't you call?" she shouted wrapping her short legs around his thighs. He sort of leaned to support her weight then made a face. Her arms around his neck almost strangled him, and he pushed her off into Rick's arms.

"Hey, man," Rick said. "How are you?"

"I've been better," Chandler admitted. "OK. Here's how it goes. The cops took me back to where we hit the guy. The crowd was still there – at least some of them were. Those left were so drunk they didn't even remember what had happened. But they did give them the name of the guy we hit and said he had already left. We found him sleeping behind a building. Homeless guy. He was fine. The booze made him so limp that the hit didn't even faze him. The cops let me go. Took me back to my car and told be to go home. It was so bizarre. The costume didn't help things, Miss Milli Mae. Thank you very kindly. I had to explain the whole story to them about the dance and our routine. It was embarrassing. So that's it. That's the whole dirty story." Chandler sunk down into the sofa in the reception room.

"Well, if you ask me," Morgan inserted. "I think you deserve to take the day off and go home. That story takes the cake. It's better than the thrown ash tray and the buffer."

61

Suzanna chewed on her finger. "I'd have to agree. You need to take the day off and rest. You're in no shape to teach lessons..."

"What lessons?" Chandler Dane's eyes narrowed.

Suzanna tittered a nervous laugh. "Yes, well. We'll just have to see about getting you a few students. Next week. Right, Mr. Hawks?" Antoine Hawks was in charge of assigning new students to teachers.

"Right! Next week." Antoine looked shocked and somehow supportive of Chandler's situation. "I have one in mind. Lettie Banks. She'd be perfect for you. Right, Mr. Gray?"

Richard Gray who started the new students nodded in agreement. "Perfect," he agreed.

Chandler got up wearily from the sofa and after a few hugs around the group left for a much needed day off. His smiling face showed his pleasure in the thought that he would actually begin teaching a student soon.

"I hope that made his day better," Antoine remarked with a grimacing look on his face as he watched the tall man walk out the door.

XI.

"Yes," Joan Ericson was saying into the phone. "Really? I had no idea. No, I don't know if it is important. Yes, I can check around for more information. What was that address again? Hmmm." Joan Ericson put down the phone and stared at the paper in front of her.

"Anything wrong, boss?" Morgan asked from her twirling desk chair. Joan was standing next to her behind the desk as Sydney tried desperately to check out her schedule. Sydney sensed the silence and moved around the corner pausing to listen to the response.

"Could you check something out for me?" Joan asked Morgan after a few seconds. "Could you check out everyone's address for me? Students and teachers alike."

"What's wrong?" Morgan said trying to catch a glimpse of the paper in Joan's hand.

"This one here sounds too familiar. I need to figure out why I know this. Get on it right away, if you can. If you don't have someone's address in the rolodex or on a student file card, ask them directly. Tell them I need to know to update records or something," Joan ordered tucking the paper into her daily calendar.

Sydney somehow felt she needed to see that paper. She didn't want to feel sneaky or look at something that didn't belong to her, but she felt the urge to know what address Joan was referring to. It must be important.

She kept her eye on Joan that day. She watched where she put her calendar and other papers. It happened when Joan had left for lunch. Morgan was looking uncomfortable behind the desk.

"What's wrong, Morgan?" Sydney asked.

"Oh, good. I didn't think anyone would come by. I have to go to the bathroom, and Joan is out to lunch. Mind answering the phones for just one moment? I'll be right back," Morgan practically ran out from behind the desk.

"Sure thing," Sydney's voice was dripping with sweetness. As soon as Morgan's back was turned, Sydney flipped open the calendar page and glanced at the address. 201 23rd Avenue South. She quickly grabbed a post-it note and jotted down the address. It must be important. Slipping the note into her pocket, she was leaning casually on the top of the desk when Morgan returned.

"No calls at all," she reported.

"Great! Thanks for the favor," Morgan sounded relieved as she regained her post behind the desk.

"No problem at all," Sydney smiled cheerfully trying not to give away too much satisfaction for the opened opportunity to check out the paper.

Sydney went back into the teacher's office and checked the roster she had clipped to her appointment book. 201 23rd Avenue South was Antoine's address. Why would that be significant? It was on her way home. Her bus passed right by that corner apartment building. Maybe she'd have to stop off and watch for a while. The building was close to the downtown area in an older section of town. She knew Antoine lived in an upper apartment in the four-plex.

That evening Sydney grabbed the bus at the usual corner then signaled for the stop on the corner of 23rd. She hoped that she would not run into Antoine. He had said he was going out to do some dancing after work, so she felt fairly safe. She asked for a transfer when she hopped off and folded it carefully before sliding it into her coat pocket.

The building was a two story stone building that showed off a classic architecture. She looked around carefully hoping not to run into someone she knew, then went up the walk to the entry way. She checked the names listed on the four mail boxes. Antoine's box was penned in heavy black marker. The darkness made reading the other names a little difficult. She put her face up to the other labels – Cox, Jameson, and Garrett. Garrett? Who lived here? Certainly not Edward. Had he moved? Was the financial situation so tight that he had sold his condo and moved to this apartment? Somehow, the whole situation seemed out of character for someone like Edward Garrett. Was he keeping a second apartment for some reason?

"Looking for someone?" The voice from over her shoulder seemed familiar.

Sydney turned abruptly and ran right into Amanda. No longer in her long fur coat, she was wearing a long black trench coat and black pants and boots. The collar of the coat was up around her head so she was almost unrecognizable.

"Oh, hello," Sydney coughed in surprise. Instead of asking what Amanda was doing here, Sydney felt obligated to stammer out an excuse for herself.

"I was looking for Antoine," she quickly answered. "He does live here, doesn't he?"

"Yes, he does. But I don't know if he's here right now. Did you ring the bell?" Amanda asked calmly knowing she was in control of this conversation.

Caught! What would she answer now? If she said no, then Amanda would press the button for her. If Antoine happened to be home, then she would have to come up with another story to satisfy both of their curiosities.

"Yes, actually I did," she lied. "I guess I'll just have to call him later or see him at the studio tomorrow." Sydney ran down the walk looking way too conspicuous in action as well as in words. As she stood at the corner hoping the next bus would come quickly, she began to ponder the event. Did Amanda Garrett live in the same building as Antoine? What did that mean? Well, it certainly meant that she and Edward were living separately. They were estranged. Did the police know that? Did they just discover this little fact and somehow find this to be a motive for murder? It was curious.

Sydney's little apartment never seemed so comforting as it did when she walked in that night and flipped the door locked behind her. She leaned her back against the door and let out a deep sigh. Murder was nothing to fool with, and she had been fooling with something today.

She ran a comfortable hot bath and began to think as she soaked in the bubbles. If Amanda was living in the same building as Antoine and hadn't bothered to tell the police about her new residence, there must be a reason. If that reason was murder, then she was in deep trouble. What should she do? If she told Joan Ericson about her discovery, she would have to admit to snooping in her private papers. If she told the police, they would want to know why she was giving them this information. Obviously it was confidential. Her only recourse was to act normally and hope Amanda and Antoine had nothing to do with Edward's death. She would have to stick to her weak and unconvincing story for being at the apartment building. She would have to play dumb until someone could give her an explanation. That explanation didn't take long in coming.

XII.

Amanda and Antoine came into the exercise class together. Never had they done that before. It was definitely for her benefit. Sydney waited at the door patiently for the door to be unlocked. The cement wall at her back seemed cold and hard as she pressed tightly against it at the sight of the two walking together holding hands.

"I understand you were looking for me," Antoine stated without an ounce of emotion.

Totally forgetting her plan to act normally, Sydney blurted out, "What's going on here?"

Antoine and Amanda didn't expect the response they received and paused to look at each other with curious frowns. They must not have anticipated Sydney's sudden boldness. They had expected the cold silence with nothing to explain. Amanda sighed deeply as she fished for her keys in her pocket and unlocked the door.

"If you think I'm not scared, you are wrong," Sydney continued following the two in the door but making sure she stood near enough to the door to make a sudden bolt if necessary. "It looks like you two killed Edward, you know. You live in the same building – maybe in the same apartment for all I know. It doesn't look good. And if I can figure this out, then the others including the police are sure to find out. It's not much of a secret anymore."

"It's not what you think... or I'm sure what the police are going to think," Amanda started.

"No way. We're just good friends, that's all," Antoine interrupted. "Hell, I'm gay. I have no interest in an intimate relationship with a woman – no offense Amanda, dear," he added patting her hands again.

She smiled. "No offense. There is nothing expected on my end." In spite of their words, there was still a syrupy sweetness between them that felt electric. Sydney felt it, but listened intently.

"Edward was having another affair. I knew there was someone else and not just a one night stand as he usually had. There was someone he was actually having a long term relationship with, but I couldn't figure out who it was. I travel a bit with my modeling and all. So it was hard to actually catch him. But I suspect it was someone from the studio. And I suspect that person may have been instrumental in his death." Amanda stopped and faltered for a second then continued. "Antoine has been a savior for me. I told him my suspicions, and he told me about an empty apartment in his building. I moved all of my things out telling Edward we needed to separate until I could figure out what to do next."

"So he actually admitted the affair?" Sydney questioned.

"No. No he never would say anything concrete. He wouldn't even give a hint as to who it was. He lied as usual and said there wasn't anyone else. But I knew better. It was way too obvious. I even suspected you for a while," Amanda paused to let that sink in.

70

"Me? Why would you ever suspect me?" Sydney pulled back in reproach. The thought of an affair with Edward Garrett gave her a creepy feeling, and she shuddered in disgust.

"You were the new one. He always tries something with the new one," Amanda let out a sound that almost sobbed.

Sydney was never so grateful for the "Little Hitler" comment as she was at this very moment. It may have saved her from an uncomfortable situation with Edward. It gave her an off limits image. She would have to thank Terry some day.

"I've been trying to find out from conversations and slipped comments staff or students might make, but so far nothing has come up to solve this mystery person's identity," Antoine added. "I'm Amanda's friend. I want to support her emotionally through this whole ordeal – the affair as well as the murder. Talk about a double tragedy of events. I don't know how much more could happen after this?"

"Well, the police could come up with the same conclusion I did and begin to suspect Amanda had something to do with the murder," Sydney put a damper on the conversation. There was a cold silence as the three of them began to settle into her suggestion.

"Yes," Amanda pondered. "That would make a bad situation even worse. I don't know if I could take something like that." Despite her aloof personality, Sydney agreed Amanda would suffer from a suggestion that she was involved. In fact her whole demeanor might fall down before them. There was only so much someone could take.

"We can't have that happen," Antoine's worried voice trailed off as he gazed into Amanda's troubled face. "There must be something we can do."

"They have Terry Crawford in for questioning," Amanda's voice sounded hopeful. "Maybe they have evidence that links him to the murder."

"His fingerprints were found on Edward's desk," Sydney stated the facts that all three knew. "That's not very much without a motive. He is a little nutty. And I think he's on drugs most of the time, but even that is a little far fetched for a motive unless you think he's Edward's new affair."

"No way," Amanda laughed. "Not even Edward is that daring. He's definitely a lady's man and not into the experimental area of a male affair. No, not Edward. I've known him long enough to be very sure of that."

Antoine's face reddened a bit as Amanda stated her opinion so boldly. "Sorry, Antoine," she stopped suddenly noting his discomfort. "It has nothing to do with you and your lifestyle. It's just I know Edward well enough to know what he is capable of, and sex with a man is definitely out for him." Antoine nodded slowly in agreement.

"Maybe Terry was involved in some other way," Sydney suggested. "Maybe they shared drugs or he was a contact for something else."

"Possible," Amanda's face brightened. "That's a possibility."

"Well, then we'll just have to find out who Edward was seeing, that's all there is to it." Sydney stated. "Maybe I can find out some things that the two of you can't. After all, no one would suspect that I would be interested in Edward's relationships, would they? I think not." Sydney knew that the two of them could be lying to her. They could be taking her into their confidence to throw her off the track, but then again all they had told her could very well be the truth as well. The only way she could find out would be to do some snooping with their blessing.

"Yeah," Antoine turned to Amanda with a new brightness in his face. "That might work. We need to spread out our efforts. A new set of ears and eyes might be just what we need. We're running out of time.

It will only be a short while before the police begin to question you about your new residence. We had better have some evidence to support your move. Otherwise there could be lots of delicate questions that we couldn't explain to them as well as we can to Sydney here."

"That's true," Amanda thought through the proposal. "We could use your help if you are willing to work with us." Amanda turned her attention to Sydney. All three nodded in agreement before another model rapped on the door.

"Oh, didn't we unlock the door?" Amanda's look was one of mock surprise. That made Sydney just a little uneasy.

XIII.

Sydney went down her list of suspects. Who would have had an affair with Edward Garrett? Suzanna Caldwell, Joan Ericson, Megan Meeker, Mimi Clark, Anna Smith, or Milli Mae Carter. Well Morgan Canfield could be ruled out unless Edward had met her before she was employed at the studio. Unlikely. Suzanna was not really Edward's type; nor was Joan Ericson. Megan Meeker? The lovely lady with the electric smile and exotic hat collection was average height with a full figure. Not Edward's type either unless he suddenly got tired of the leggy model look. Mimi Clark was too short and too encumbered with ex-husband and young child baggage. Although Sydney did notice that whenever Mimi brought her daughter into the studio, Edward took great joy in entertaining her with colors and books. It was somewhat out of character for him to get down to the child level. Maybe he actually was more of a child and could relate more to that age on an equal level. The child aspect was something she would have to consider.

Milli Mae had a personality that would appeal to Edward – blunt, energetic, and a real spitfire. He would find that a challenge. Possible although she was too short for his taste. Anna Smith seemed to rub Edward the wrong way. She was young but too matronly for him Sydney concluded. They did seem to have heated words the other day though when he put her on the buffer. Why would he pick her out for such a task unless he was trying to show her who was boss? Was there anyone else? Sydney couldn't think of anyone off hand.

Craig Fritz came in to teach a few lessons. He had a few students who were devoted to him and had been for years. Although he didn't fit into the normal dance studio staff cookie cutter, he must have at one point. He must have just plain gotten tired of the stuff that was going on and just kept in it enough to get the thrill of dancing and nothing more.

"Hi Craig," Sydney greeted him as he danced his way out onto the floor.

"Hi doll," Craig grinned with a flirty glance at her. "Want to dance. Samba?"

"Sure," Sydney smiled broadly and began a lively step across the floor with Craig trying some of his usual showier steps. When they slowed at the end of the dance, Sydney began with a compliment. "That was nice. Say Craig, how long have you taught here at the studio?"

"Eight years now – give or take a few years," he laughed. "Sometimes it seems longer, other days it feels shorter. Of course I was just a child when I started." He laughed again at his joke. "I was actually in high school when I began teaching."

"So what do you think of Edward's murder? It's all the conversation around here lately. I have to admit, I'm too new here to have any opinion," Sydney rambled on a bit trying to act innocent in her questions.

"Puzzling. Yes, definitely puzzling. Eddie G. and I shared a lot of things," he laughed again. "We both were good dancers. We both shared ladies. We followed the same circle of friends."

"Oh, really," Sydney couldn't quite picture Edward and Craig in the same group, but she wanted to know more. "Who did you both hang out with?"

"You know, all the important people. TV people, movie people, all the wealthy ones at the top," Craig bragged puffing out his chest.

"Like who? Who would I know?" Sydney kept up the conversation without trying to seem too impressed.

"Well, no one you would know." Craig scowled slightly that she wasn't ogling more over his name dropping.

"I know lots of important people too. Who do you know?" Sydney batted her eyelashes in mock humor.

Craig suddenly stopped short and opened his mouth. Nothing came out at first. Should he try to impress this woman or just move on to another subject? He plunged forward. "Eddie G. and I always date the same women. You know, the model types. They just fall all over us." He stood taller and glared down at her waiting for her approval.

"Wow," she cocked her head to the side. "Who did you share? Amanda?"

"Naw, she's too much of a scarecrow for me," Craig smirked.

Never had Sydney heard Amanda referred to as a "scarecrow". She just looked back up into his face and waited for an answer.

"Well, we are currently – I guess he is no longer current – but we were both seeing the same woman until he was murdered." Craig hesitated to mention a name.

"Unless you tell me who she is, I can't say that I believe you," Sydney turned with a flounce. She knew the comment would really get to Craig. Either he would dismiss her without another thought, or he would start thinking about her comments and come running with a name. Which would it be?

It wasn't long before Sydney received her answer. She was outside sitting on the stone wall that surrounded the plaza with a sack of food from McDonalds when she felt a whirl of wind fly by. What in the world could that be? Sipping on her diet coke she looked up to see Craig teetering on a unicycle.

"Care for a ride on my shoulders?" he sat on top of the seat rolling slightly back and forth.

"You must be kidding! I'm afraid of heights, actually," Sydney swallowed her mouthful of fries and gazed in amazement at the spectacle in front of her.

Craig had on a hat that he held with both hand balancing with his elbows out to the side. "Your question about my newest lady love can be answered with a question," he grinned.

"And what question would that be?" Sydney wasn't happy that her action had only brought a riddle instead of an outright answer.

"She's someone you would least suspect. Someone no one would suspect. Edward didn't know I was seeing her until the night of his death. We both found out about the other in an unusual way that I'm not about to tell you." Craig was about to ride off when Sydney asked, "How did he find out about you?"

Craig couldn't resist. He wheeled his cycle around in a circle. "I don't know how he found out. I just know he did because he called me into his office at the end of the day, and we had it out."

"What do you mean you had it out?" Sydney's voice was low.

"He called me into the inner sanctuary and told me he knew about me and this certain lady. He told me I was to stop seeing her because she was his. I don't know how he found out, but I laughed in his face. He didn't like that. Began to sputter like he does with his cheeks all puffed out and that scowl on his face. He has no idea how funny that looks. I began to laugh again and he threw me out. I laughed all the way home." Craig leaned his head back and began to laugh again. "I guess he lost out. Not my fault someone went in and shot him. Not my style. I'd rather laugh in his face."

Craig flashed a grin, raised his eyebrows and pedaled off in the direction of the studio.

Sydney wondered why police hadn't pulled Craig in. His prints were obviously in Edward's office as well as Terry's. Maybe someone saw Craig in the office and had already reported his presence that night. Craig must have left before the others giving him a timeline alibi. He certainly could have gone back, but why. He had bested Edward and he knew it. That was more revenge than a bullet. The clues to the woman's identity were no better than before. Someone she wouldn't suspect? Who would that be?

XIV.

Sydney finished her lunch and wandered back into the studio. The downtown air felt hazy and cloudy without any brightness or warmth to still the shiver that surged through her body. Craig was no longer in the studio. He would come and go as he pleased — marking out times that weren't already scheduled with a standing appointment.

As she walking in, Morgan motioned her to the desk. "You've got a call. Some guy who's been calling a couple of times already today. You want to take it?"

Some guy? Who could that be? "Sure," Sydney went to the back teachers' office and picked up the blinking line.

"Sydney?" the voice was familiar.

"Who is this?" Sydney asked.

"It's Terry."

"Terry? Where are you? What happened to you?" Why was Terry calling her? Sydney thought.

"I'm still at the police station. They found my finger prints on the top of Edward's desk. You gotta help me. Listen I know we've had our differences lately, but you're my only friend. I need your help," Terry pleaded.

"OK. Tell me, Terry, why were you in Edward's office that night?" Sydney felt sorry for the guy. If she was his only friend then he was in big trouble.

Terry hesitated. "He called me into his office for a meeting."

"About what?" Sydney felt Terry hesitate again. "Listen if I'm your friend and you need my help, you need to tell me the truth. You have to tell me everything."

"I know. OK. He called me in because someone suspected me of stealing. Taking money from purses in the teachers' office," Terry spoke boldly.

"So did you? Did you take money from the purses?" Sydney already knew the answer to her question, but she wanted to know if Terry was telling her the truth.

"Yes, yes I was. I'm not making anything these days," he sounded angry and defiant. "Let's face it, the studio pay sucks. But I'm committed to this business and this dancing. I'm determined to prove to everyone that I'm good at teaching. I personally think I'm great at this stuff. I'm an actor. I can handle the dancing, the teaching, and the talking part. I just want to show Suzanna I'm the best she's got, that's all," Terry skillfully sidestepped the question with a truthful admittance. Defiant but honest.

"Thanks for the truth. So you think Suzanna is the one out to get you?" Sydney was curious.

"Absolutely. She's been out to get me from day one. That's why the police have those pictures of me," Terry sounded sane enough.

"What pictures would that be?" Sydney hesitated.

"I sent Edward some, well, how can I say this tactfully…indiscrete photos of myself before I even started at the studio. I thought they might show my dance background I guess. He never mentioned them but I guess he kept them or something because they police found them on his desk. That was so long ago, I didn't even remember that I sent those things. What can I say?" Terry rambled a bit.

"So you think Suzanna put those pictures on the desk?" Sydney was trying to follow the logic of this.

"Who else? Who else is out to get me but that woman? She's always hated me. It had to be her. Edward never mentioned those when we had our little meeting. I swear they weren't there," Terry was getting frustrated.

"So tell me how the meeting happened? When did you go into the office?"

"Suzanna told me Edward wanted a meeting with me. So I sat out in the reception area for a couple of minutes. He was yelling at someone else. Then Craig stormed out and headed out the front door.

So I went in, and we actually had a nice calm talk about the situation. I was a little irritated when I left because he mentioned calling in the police, but it wasn't a yelling match or anything. It was pretty matter of fact. There you have it." Terry related his story.

"And you're sure Craig left after his meeting?"

"Absolutely. He couldn't wait to get to the door," Terry recalled.

"What about after your meeting? Who was left when you were done?" Sydney racked her brain for answers.

"No one. Everyone was gone. That's why I'm a suspect I guess. I was the last to see him alive except for the real killer of course," Terry related.

"What time was that?"

"About quarter to eleven. I was in there for about forty five minutes hashing out all my woes, begging for more students, more money – you know that kind of thing." Terry could talk forever about any subject that was for sure.

"OK. What do you want me to do?" Sydney didn't want to tell him that she was already trying to find out a few things for Amanda and Antoine.

"Listen. Find out who else was there. Get me another suspect," Terry begged. "There had to be someone else."

Sydney didn't want him to get his hopes up. She didn't want to tell him she was looking into the possibility of an affair. She was just a dance teacher who didn't even feel like a very good friend to this man at the moment. He was certainly a thief and a druggie and who knows what else. He did make the perfect suspect in spite of his vehement denial. Terry was volatile and unpredictable as well as a great actor who could lie convincingly. He hadn't lied to her just now about his stealing that was for sure, but what about the content of his meeting with Edward? It was hard to believe Edward could go from a screaming maniac with Craig to a calm collected man discussing a crime with Terry. It didn't seem possible. Edward could be puzzling and moody, but to switch on and off like that in a matter of minutes was difficult to imagine.

Sydney put down the phone and sat for a moment. It would be so easy if she could just believe Terry had committed this murder. Something was wrong with the picture though.

As she sat thinking through the possibilities, Megan Meeker ambled in humming a catchy tune. She bopped to her own music.

Carrying a pair of glass disco shoes, she went over to an electrical outlet and plugged them in.

"Just have to plug in my shoes," Megan joked. The shoes were high platforms, clear with flashing lights inside that sparkled with each step to the ground. "Can you believe I wear these things?"

Megan wore a silky blue two piece skirt and blouse with a matching blue tam on her head. The tam sparkled with a glittering bauble on the side. Her makeup was impeccable as usual and her full lips a bright red.

"Listen, Megan," Sydney decided if she was to discover who had killed Edward she would have to take someone else into her confidence. "I know you've been here a long time. Do you think Terry killed Edward?"

Megan hesitated. "Terry is the oddest person I have ever met. He gives me the creeps with his slimy appearance and awful odor. It is positively hideous. But did he kill Edward? I don't know. It would be nice if I thought he did because then there wouldn't be someone else out there not to trust. I'd just as soon not trust Terry than someone else. You know what I mean."

"Yeah, that's true. But do you think Edward was having an affair? Was he cheating on Amanda?"

"Was he cheating on Amanda? Of course. Eddie G. always cheated on his women. When he married Amanda I was thrilled. She was different – elegant yet down to earth. A real tell it like it is person who was not content to be one of his airhead bimbos. That's why he married her, I think. She was different than the women he was usually attracted to. She actually had a brain and personality. I was proud of him for finally admitting that he loved someone. I thought she was perfect for him. I didn't feel particularly close to her, but I thought she was great for Edward. But would he cheat on her? That was the nature of the beast. That was Edward Garrett. He was a cheater and a moody despicable man, but somehow had charisma. He could make you love dance and life and everything else the world had to offer. That was the cool part about the man. I admired him in spite of his faults – and he certainly had those."

Sydney pondered her words. "OK. If Edward was having an affair with someone from the studio, who would that person be?"

"That is a more difficult question. I think in his own way Edward cared about each person on his staff. Was he above having an affair with any one of us? No. He would have jumped at the chance. But someone to jeopardize his relationship with Amanda? He wasn't that stupid, and we all aren't his type. We all aren't worth the price. If he was having an affair, it would have to be with someone very different. More his standard model type but with an independent air to her – someone who would challenge him. That's the only draw that would keep him hooked." Megan had hit the nail on the head. The person would have to be his type yet different. She would have to be unreachable. A challenge.

"So who's unreachable?" Sydney asked.

"Beats me," Megan just shook her head. "Make sure these shoes stay plugged in will you? Don't let anyone pull them off this outlet." Megan flashed a smile and walked out of the teachers' office.

Sydney made her way out to the reception desk to recheck her schedule and warm up on the dance floor. Megan was standing at the desk and picking through some photos of the routine at Frankie's.

"Who took these?" Sydney asked peering over the desktop.

"Someone from Frankie's took them and these from last week as well. They just dropped them off," Morgan chimed.

"No matter what Edward said about us, we are absolutely the most beautiful looking dancers in the world," Megan stated. "Look at those lines, and the costumes in spite of being totally uncomfortable look great on us." She was holding up a photo of the group doing a long leggy line. "I am not fat."

"What! Edward Garrett told you that you were fat?" Morgan's face twisted into shock. Morgan was a woman who was a little stockier. Her round cheeks and dishwater blond hair hanging limply around her face gave her a plain Nordic look. "How could that man ever say such a thing?"

"Beats me. Here's the proof. We are absolutely lovely women," Megan restated firmly.

Sydney picked up the stack of pictures and after agreeing with Megan's assessment, began to page through the ones from last week. It gave her a creepy feeling to see Edward out on that floor with Amanda smiling and moving. Now that he was no longer, it felt as if something had snapped. Amanda was stoic and crisp in her lines and facial expressions, but Edward was as animated as usual. His mouth opened in one photo as he moved into a roll out position with his partner. They were the only couple dancing in that show. The background was dark and hazy but there were some of the staff members circled round the floor watching the show. She could make out Craig leaning against the back wall, and Chandler with Rick Krist in another picture. The photographer had brought over only the show pictures, but maybe there were others taken before and after the show. Maybe there would be one of the mystery lady. She would have to check with Frankie's later.

Megan greeted her student sitting in the reception area. He was young with a bright colored multi print shirt. She picked up a black folder with his name printed across the front.

"Good day, Mr. Hanson. And how are you?" A huge smile pressed across her face. She didn't wait for an answer and simply turned toward the ballroom.

Mr. Hanson only nodded shyly and followed her out to the floor for his lesson.

Sydney ambled back to the teachers' office. Suzanna and Carson Hunter were sitting close together behind her desk. Suzanna was singing a little song in Carson's ear as he held a dance program on his lap. "Pruney face! You've got the cutest little pruney face." It was the song they sang before each lesson with Angela Pratt. Angela Pratt was a tiny wrinkled old woman who had come in weekly for years. Carson

Hunter had recently inherited Angela as his student. Craig taught her for years, but Craig was unreliable and often didn't show up for her afternoon lessons. She had complained personally to Edward who had made the new assignment.

Angela Pratt was not any easy woman to teach. She was impatient and expected the full attentions of her teacher. Carson Hunter was a well educated yet quiet man who knew just about all you could ever hope to know about the techniques of dance. He was not, however, a person who gushed attention on his students. It just wasn't nor would it ever be his nature. Suzanna sang this little "Pruney Face" (sung to the tune of "Baby Face") song before each lesson to get him inspired. Whether it inspired Carson was a matter of opinion. Sydney didn't see a whole lot of difference between the pre-Carson person and the post-Carson person, but then again maybe it was an internal transformation thing.

Suzanna, usually a person who was content to watch and observe, showed a unique side to her personality when she sang her little song. Sydney was more interested in watching Suzanna sing than trying to see the reaction of Carson to this antic.

"You will come out on this lesson and give us some flashy, wonderful new material to work on, won't you?" Carson asked in a somber monotone.

Suzanna became unexpectedly animated as she answered brightly, "You bet. Absolutely. It will be extraordinary and unbelievable!" She stood up and hit a dance pose flinging her head back to dramatize her motion.

Sydney hadn't seen Suzanna so uninhibited – well, ever. She usually joked around with Carson before lessons, but this was not typical of Suzanna to so freely spotlight her own charming personality. Usually she hid her expression behind her hand and her slight size 4 figure behind the drums in the ballroom. Today she wore a handkerchief cut dress of printed navy and had left her owl sized glasses on her desk. Her usually nondescript face was beautifully blushed and her eyes were wide and perfectly made up with a deep tinted eye shadow. She smiled brightly at Carson then greeted Sydney with a wiggle of her fingers.

"My, you're in a great mood today," Sydney commented.

"It's anticipating pruney face's lesson," she flung her hair from side to side and leaned over Carson to flash him a vibrant grin.

A slow smile crept over Carson's usually expressionless face. He was amused as well. Carson was a college flower child during the Vietnam War complete with the wire rims and long ponytail. Today, however, he looked more like a college professor. His hair was short, and he wore his uniform, as Sydney commonly referred to his gray vest over darker gray dress trousers. He still wore the wire rims and a neatly trimmed dark mustache. Carson Hunter faded into the background when with a group, but there was something endearing and special about Carson that made everyone who met him call him "friend". You could say that Carson Hunter and Edward Garrett were about as opposite as any two men could be. Although they were fairly close in age, they were in different generations and different phases of life. Well, Edward was in no phase of life anymore. Sydney frowned unexpectedly at this thought and moved on to arranging her day.

Sydney sauntered out to the dance floor to work on a few new steps in Cha Cha. Carson followed her out leading a tiny wrinkled Angela Pratt. Angela was in heaven as Carson took her into his arms for a slow Rumba. A wide smile seemed painted on her face as she closed her eyes and swayed to the music. Suzanna slid into her spot behind the drums and watched patiently for the warm up dance to end. She let

Carson demonstrate a few patterns and reflect a take charge attitude before stepping out to the floor.

"Good day, Miss Pratt. How are you enjoying your lessons with Mr. Hunter?" Suzanna waited for a response.

"Oh, he is an excellent teacher," Angela gushed turning her pruney face toward Carson for an approving look.

Carson's mouth turned up into a tight lipped smile. He nodded his head slightly as if agreeing with all she was saying.

"Mr. Hunter and I have been discussing several special dance moves we would like you to try," Suzanna continued. "We feel you are ready for some new dance material that will challenge you a bit more." Waiting for a response from Angela, Suzanna continued as Angela became quite giddy. "We were thinking a Paso Doble might challenge you with some wonderful new steps. You do understand that Paso Doble is a very advanced dance – the bull fighter's dance. The man is the matador and the woman the cape swirling from side to side."

Again Suzanna waited for Angela to take in a gasp of air as if quite honored that they would consider the Paso Doble for her. Then Suzanna demonstrated a few movements with Carson for Angela. Carson began with several side moving quick foot pounding steps to the side then swooped Suzanna across in front of his body from side to side as if she were his cape. It was quite impressive. Angela's eyes grew bigger and her face crinkled into a mass of crevices as she smiled widely.

Sydney moved across the floor to one of the glass tables that circled the front of the windows along the east side of the ballroom floor. She took a seat and spread her dance step lists for a better view. Her mind wandered from the Angela Pratt lesson, and she began to focus on her Cha Cha notes.

Richard Gray moved out to the dance floor with the grace of a high class waiter – straight as an arrow and smooth as someone balancing a tray of filled to the brim drinks. He appeared not to pay attention to anyone else out on the floor. Staring into the mirror, he held his arms out to the side and swayed. His eyes seemed to be looking at something far beyond the scope of the mirror image. Then just as suddenly as he began, he peered into the mirror and spotted Sydney seated at the table. With a wave of his hand, he acknowledged her. Then he continued with his own dance moves in a sweeping and elegant gesture.

Sydney looked around for her pen to take some notes. Nothing. She impatiently got up and walked through the reception area hoping to snag a loose pen from the desk as she passed.

Mrs. Lang was in the lobby bending Morgan's ear. Morgan was perched on the couch next to the elderly Mrs. Lang with her head close. "They actually suggested that I would come back to the studio after the party and pull a gun to shoot the man. Can you image?"

Morgan shook her head sadly in agreement that begged more information. Mrs. Lang obliged with a louder explanation. "I guess that conversation we had last week was something of a news item to those talking to the cops," Mrs. Lang's voice was pitching higher so the studio ears would be sure to hear. "I told them I haven't even been to a party in years because I don't drive at night...period!" With a harrumph she settled herself into the seat cushions and primly twisted her hands in her lap. "Besides, my neighbor gentleman was over for a late supper. He verified my whereabouts."

XV.

Rick Krist and Chandler Dane were sitting at the tables in the ballroom with Megan Meeker leaning over staring intently into

96

Chandler's closed eyes. "He'll do it!" Rick was saying with a smirk of satisfaction on his face.

"No really," Megan continued. "The idea is fabulous. We can do a Swing to 'Splish Splash I was taking a bath'. You hide in the back room over there and when the introduction is over, you come out wearing just a towel." Megan's sapphire blue dress was highlighting the blue in her eyes although Chandler was pretending not to notice by squeezing his lids closed. "Why me?" he was muttering as Megan continued to outline her idea for their next dance routine. "The best part is when you come out – wrapped only in a towel as I was describing – scrubbing your back with a toilet bowl brush." At that Rick and Megan howled with laughter.

"Tell me Miss Meeker," Chandler said with an emphasis on the "Miss", "why you are intent on humiliating me and not Rick here. Wouldn't it be even funnier if this tub of lard comes out in a towel?"

"Heavens no!" Megan started in surprise. "Why ever would you say that?"

Rick Krist looked horrified. "I don't think so. You're perfect. People go for the lean look." Rick's expression turned to a chuckling.

97

"Right!" Chandler shook his head as Megan whispered in a low voice, "You are just so much funnier than you will ever know, Chandler."

"He'll think about it," Rick answered her back as she straightened the patterned blue scarf that wrapped around her head. She flashed a big smile before leaving the two to discuss the idea.

Sydney grabbed Megan to see if she was interested in lunch over at Frankie's. She was dying to get a look at those pictures from the nights of the shows. Megan could talk a cat into water and would surely be an asset in her attempt to find the photographer.

"I have a lesson coming up, but if you can wait until later, I'd love to do lunch," Megan flashed a charming smile as she grabbed a student's program and began to page through front to back.

"Let me check my schedule and get back with you, but I think I could do it later," Sydney pondered. She leaned over the desk top to read the daily schedule from her up-side-down position and straighten when Morgan gave her a nasty look. "Yup, later is good!" she responded.

Sydney wandered out to the ballroom to sit with Chandler and Rick. A few questions couldn't hurt.

"Mind if I sit with you?" Sydney fingered the back of a chair.

"Don't tell me you're here to talk me into that ridiculous bath idea too," Chandler groaned without looking up.

"No way! Have no plans to get you into a towel and toilet bowl brush. I just wanted to talk a little about Edward. Curiosity you know," Sydney eased into the subject.

"Take a seat," Rick Krist bellowed.

"So who do you think did it?" Sydney quickly sat and leaned in a little.

"Subtle, subtle," Chandler cooed opening his eyes and tilting his head toward her.

"Could be the grieving widow, or the jilted girl friend, or some disgruntled student …," Rick listed.

"Or some disgruntled teacher…," Chandler added.

"So you think Edward had a jilted girl friend?" Sydney directed at Rick.

"Edward always had a jilted girl friend. No news there."

"What about you, Rick? You let your temper boil over occasionally," Sydney got to her point as quickly as possible.

"Temper? Me?" But Rick was anything but offended. He was smiling and laughing as was Chandler who began to find this humorous.

"Sure I have a temper. But it's only directed to slimy characters like Terry Crawford." Rick saw the point Sydney was making clearly.

"And you don't consider Edward 'slimy'?" Sydney pulled back with a perplexed look on her face.

"There's 'slimy' and there's 'slimy'. If you get what I mean," Rick emphasized every word in his sentences.

"I suppose …," Sydney pondered. "Give me more."

"Edward was not a nice person. He cheated his employees. He cheated his wife. He cheated his students. Yet somehow, he was not a bad guy. He had charisma and charm and was the envy of everyone here that he got away with all the crap. I don't know how he did it, do you? I guess it was pure and simple. He was in control. He intimidated everyone he met with his power to control. Everyone just went along because he had the power to charm you then knock you down all at the same time. It was a weird combination. No, I didn't have the hate for Edward to kill him. I had sort of an awe – an admiration - that he could get away with all he did. But someone else obviously didn't share my awe. He crossed the line with someone, and that someone crossed back." Rick finished his analysis and both Sydney and Chandler nodded in agreement. He was right. Edward was in charge of everyone here.

Those he couldn't control he made his project. They became his focus. Just like Sydney with her "little Hitler" comment. That just spurred him on all the more. She would have become a project if he had lived. But there was someone else who had challenged him as well. And that someone had become tired of being controlled and found the only way to get free was to kill him. So who was that person?

Megan, Carson and Mimi were out on the floor with students. The music was playing a fast Mambo. Carson began to perk up. The music seemed to lift him past his usual low key demeanor. Megan noticed his spirited movements and coaxed her student to dance toward Carson and his partner. The two couples began to challenge each other with glancing looks and grinning expressions. Mimi's student, a new student who was having trouble just moving his feet at all, wanted desperately to join in. But the speed and quick movements were just not there for him yet. Mimi squealed with delight at the sight of Carson spinning, and Megan waving her skirt on a turn.

"This is what dancing is all about," Sydney thought as she smiled. The air was electric.

No one heard the bell at the front door clang. The music was too loud and the entertainment was too engrossing. Suddenly Morgan's voice could be heard above the sound.

"No way. You can't go in there," she was shouting as she held back a big burly man dressed in a black leather jacket and torn jeans.

"I can go where I want, lady," he yelled back and tried to get around her. But Morgan stood her ground proving she was not one to be reckoned with. Not a tiny lady by any means, she was husky and determined. When he tried to roll around her, she grasped a hold of his leather collar and pulled roughly at his neck. "Call the police," she yelled to Joan Ericson who was just coming in the front door.

With lightening fast reflexes, Joan reached over the desk and began to dial.

"I'm out a here," the man growled and twisting away headed for the door. He looked back briefly as if to challenge Joan to actually make the call then glanced back to the ballroom where his eyes narrowed. Then he was gone.

Morgan had been thrown to the floor, and a shaken Joan was still holding the phone while trying to reach a hand toward Morgan to help her up. Rick and Chandler were over there in a second pulling the woman to her feet. Her face was red and angry.

"How dare that man think he can get by me," Morgan roared. "How dare he!"

The two promptly got Morgan seated behind the desk and were handing her the pop can she stashed behind the counter.

"Settle, settle," Rick Krist was advising as he took the phone from Joan's hand and placed it back in its cradle.

"Who the hell was that?" Morgan demanded.

"Mimi's husband," Joan answered in a whisper.

"Ex-husband," Rick corrected.

"Any question as to why he's the ex," Chandler added.

"Oh, give me a break! How could that sweet little lady ever marry that big oaf anyway?" Morgan bellowed.

"Try maybe shot gun wedding?" Chandler ventured.

Mimi stuck her head around the corner of the divider. Her face was bright red, and she was wide eyed with fright. "Sorry about that, Morgan... I mean Miss Canfield," Mimi's tiny voice was apologetic. "I'm so sorry."

"No, I'm sorry," Morgan said. "I'm sorry you ever were married to that guy. Thank God you're out of that now."

Mimi nodded her head then turned back to her lesson. Morgan rolled her eyes and took another gulp from her pop can.

XVI.

Sydney and Megan meandered down the street to Frankie's. Lunch at Frankie's wasn't that great. It was a bar – a disco – so the food was in the burger and fries category. When they entered, the place was dark and sparsely occupied. There were a few heavily made up ladies in the corner chomping down on a big plate of fries with a pitcher of beer. There were a few regulars at the bar drinking their lunch. This was not the place that prominent business people from the downtown skyscrapers went for lunch. Besides it was too late for normal lunches. Studio time was different than regular time. Lunch at the studio was at 4:00 PM and not at noon. So by the time they got around to lunch, most places where pretty much deserted.

Megan slid into a booth near the front, and Sydney took the spot across from her. A waitress came over with menus. "Get you something to drink?" she asked.

"No thanks! Working," Megan explained as she grabbed her menu.

"Excuse me." Sydney raised her voice toward the waitress as she was turning to leave. "We're from the dance studio that does the shows."

The waitress nodded as if she knew at least what Sydney was talking about.

"Someone brought in some photos of some of the shows. Do you know who that would be?" Sydney asked.

The waitress at first looked puzzled but then said she would check into it and get back to her. She moved up to the bar, motioned for the bartender to come close, then began to point toward their booth. They both nodded their heads and spoke briefly.

When the waitress came back for their order she began with, "The bartender is checking it out with the management. I'll probably have an answer for you when I bring your order. I remember someone showing me a couple of pictures the other night. So we'll try to get a name for you." Then she took their order.

They enjoyed their burgers and sodas and talked about the afternoon disturbance. "Mimi lives with her mom now," Megan was saying. "That guy is really something - as big and mean as they get. Mimi married him when she was in high school. She was pregnant and didn't see any other way out. I suppose back then she thought she loved him. They seem different in high school and then unfortunately they grow up. Or maybe the problem is they don't ever grow up." They both laughed at that.

The waitress came over with a piece of paper. This is the name of the photographer. Frankie's hires him to occasionally come in and take some promo shots for ads and stuff. He's usually in every evening - hanging out if you want to find him. Otherwise here is his card with his business number and address."

They thanked her, paid their bill and left for the studio.

Five minutes until her lesson. Sydney grabbed the folders for her evening lessons and then pulled the business card from her pocket. Finding the phone in the back teachers' office free, she dialed the number. She got an answering machine, but decided to leave a message with her name and mission. "If you're free tonight and plan on hanging out at Frankie's…I'd like to take a look at the whole stack of photos from those two evenings. Hope to see you later."

She taught a lesson and then looked around for someone to go with her to Frankie's later that evening. She didn't really want to go in there alone. Richard was passing, so she decided to ask him.

"Sorry," he said. "I love to go out dancing but Darian is away on a flight, and I never go out without her."

"How often does she fly?" Sydney asked.

"Oh, a couple of times a week at least. She's had a lot of longer trips lately. They pay better you know. More layover time. Some of the other flight attendants have kids and all, so it's no problem for us when she has to do the longer times." Richard was so matter of fact. His face showed no expression at all. Ever the professional. Tonight he was dressed in a navy blue suit with a pale blue vest. Everything was wrinkle free in stark contrast to Terry who always looked like he had spent the last week in the same suit.

Chandler came up just as Sydney was about to go out on the floor for her next lesson.

"Need someone to go to Frankie's with you? I'd be happy to go. I've got no plans," he offered.

"Thanks! That would be great," Sydney punched him in the arm and headed out to the floor. Problem solved.

Frankie's was crowded already at 10:15. With no Edward to call an impromptu meeting, it was certainly easy to get out earlier than usual. Sydney and Chandler squeezed through the crowd. She had explained to him that she was trying to find a photographer by the name of Tom Potter. Did he know who that was?

"No," Chandler admitted. "I know lots of people, but I don't know a Tom Potter."

They spotted Craig Fritz over in the corner surrounded by a few leggy ladies. Certainly Craig would know who the man was. So they made their way over to his corner.

"Sorry to interrupt," Sydney began.

"No problem, Doll. What can I do for you? Wanna dance?" Craig held his hand out and motioned to the floor. In spite of the crowds in the bar area, the floor was almost empty. The music wasn't exactly danceable just yet. The DJ must wait for a certain hour to pour on the popular stuff.

"Sure." She smiled at Chandler with a half hearted grin and moved out to the floor. Craig began with a fast Hustle. Sydney wanted to talk with him about this Tom guy so she motioned to slow it down a bit, and he promptly moved into a close dance hold.

108

"Do you know a photographer named Tom Potter," Sydney spoke above the din of the music.

"What?" He leaned closer.

"Do you know a photographer named Tom Potter," Sydney repeated.

"Ah, yeah. I think so. Short red curly hair. Kind of hangs out around the bar with his camera around his neck," Craig replied. "Why? You dumping me for some short guy who doesn't dance?"

Sydney laughed. "He took some pictures of the routines, and I want to see the whole lot of them, that's all. Could you point him out to me if you happen to see him?"

"Sure thing," Craig pulled her back to the corner where Chandler was still standing trying to talk to the ladies Craig had left. Craig saddled up to one of them, put his arm around her shoulder and asked her for the next dance.

"Come on," Sydney grabbed Chandler's arm. "Let's mingle." When she got him to a quieter spot in the room she described Tom Potter as best she could from Craig's words. The best shot they had in recognizing Tom Potter seemed to be the camera around the neck.

No one with a camera emerged the whole evening. Maybe he hadn't gotten her message, or maybe he already had previous plans. As it got closer to closing, Chandler offered her a ride home.

"Thanks, but I think I'd feel safer on the bus," Sydney giggled. Chandler hung his head. "No, just kidding," she added. "A ride would be great."

Sydney glanced around the crowded room one last time. Craig had his back to them with some poor girl pressed against the wall. It was hard to see who it was, but she had the same dark sleek hair of Darian Gray.

Sydney turned to grab Chandler's arm. He was looking around in the other direction. "Hey, isn't that Darian Gray?" she asked him.

"Where?" Chandler's head moved from side to side.

"Over there talking to Craig." They both swung around toward the corner, but there was no one there. "Couldn't be. Must be mistaken. Richard said she was on a flight tonight." Sydney shook her head and blinked her tired eyes, trying to get the moisture back to soothe her dry contact lenses. She was always seeing people who looked like someone else at Frankie's – Terry, Darian, and Tom Potter. But no one was ever really who they appeared to be.

"Everyone looks alike around here," Chandler was saying. That was so true. Everyone looked the same. But no curly red haired short guy with a camera slung around his neck that was for sure.

XVII

The next morning Sydney went in early for exercise. Somehow it seemed strange without Eddie G. The class had dwindled despite Amanda's connections to the modeling world. For Sydney the change was good. Amanda led a good workout in a precise and orderly fashion without all the moodiness and hoopla that Edward provided. Maybe that's why the other models found it boring. They liked the eccentric atmosphere that he had provided.

Afterwards Sydney called Tom Potter's number again. This time she got an answer from a real live person. "Tom Potter?" she responded to the voice.

"That's me," he replied.

"This is Sydney Monroe. I left a message on your machine yesterday regarding some photos you took at Frankie's."

"Oh, yeah. I got your message and tried to find you last night, but I guess we never crossed paths," he laughed slightly.

"You were there?" Sydney felt a wave of surprise.

"Sure. Where were you? I thought someone might point me out. Someone from the bar – they all know me," he sounded confused.

"Yeah, well, I guess not. Could we meet today? Lunch?" she suggested.

"I'm busy all day with several shoots, but I could drop off the stack of photos I have at the studio again. I park there as my dark room is downtown not too far away. Maybe drop them off soon. I have to head out to a scheduled appointment in about ten minutes."

"That sounds great. I'll be waiting at the front desk," Sydney offered knowing no one else was in this early. She would be the only one around for about another hour or so.

"See you then," he sounded friendly and upbeat.

Sydney stood at the desk peering out the door looking for a short curly red haired guy. Crowds of people waited by the elevator doors every couple of minutes waiting to go up to their parked cars.

A tall slender dark haired man walked in. He had a boyish face with a mustache to make him look more professional she guessed.

"Sydney Monroe?" he asked.

"You can't be Tom Potter," she hesitated.

112

"The one and only," he grinned.

"No wonder I never found you last night. Someone told me to look for a short curly red haired man. You look nothing like that," she laughed.

He chuckled along with her nodding his head. "No I don't come close to that description. Who gave that one to you?"

"Craig Fritz. Do you know him?" Sydney guessed that he and Craig had never met.

"Sure. I know Craig real well. He's always asking me to take pictures of him when he dances. Never buys anything, but I still take the shots anyway. Maybe some day I'll get a customer from those. Who knows. If you find any shots that you want, let me know, and I'll sell you those copies. They might look good here in the studio," Tom Potter looked around at the stark walls in the lobby. There was a bulletin board that displayed schedules and upcoming events as well as accomplishments of some of the studio's most distinguished students. Otherwise, the walls seemed bare. Maybe some photos would give people something to look at as they waited for lessons. Sydney would have to suggest that to Amanda.

"Sure thing. I think that's a great suggestion," Sydney said grabbing the stack of photos in the manila envelop that Tom held out to her. "I'll get the ones I don't want back to you soon – a couple of days or so. I'll give you a call."

He nodded and left.

She sat down on the sofa and began to look through the stack. It included the same photos of the dancers she had looked at previously as well some candid shots of the crowd. The first stack was from the show Edward and Amanda had done previously. She noticed several of the studio staff and students in the crowd photos. Nothing unusual there. The second stack was from the show they performed after the murder. She quickly checked to see if Terry was in any of those photos just to prove to herself that he hadn't been a mirage. He wasn't in any of the pictures, however. There didn't seem to be anything amiss in these either. She pulled out a few of the photos from the crowd pictures that showed staff and students for possible purchase to add to the event board then put the rest back into the envelop.

The bell clanged and Mimi came in wrapped in a head scarf and sun glasses. Her well worn coat was buttoned up around her neck. She hesitated then turned to Sydney.

"Is Antoine in? He usually comes in early for exercise class doesn't he?" she slouched down a bit making her even smaller than she already was.

"He didn't come in today. Sorry," Sydney twisted her mouth into a grimace and shook her head.

"How about Suzanna?" It was then that Sydney noticed the slight discoloration around her mouth and cheeks.

"What's happened to you?" Sydney leapt to her feet and ran to Mimi peering into her face.

"Don't look at me!" Mimi had a wet tear rolling down below her sunglasses. Then she unwrapped her scarf and took off her glasses. Mimi's face was bruised, her eyes were blackened and her scalp had patches of hair missing. There was a bruised ring around her neck. "My ex was at my house when I got home last night from work. I can't very well teach looking like this, now can I?"

Sydney put her arms around the slouching woman, but Mimi pulled back. "My body looks as bad as my face and feels even worse," she explained with a slight hesitating sob.

"I hope you filed a police report against that guy," Sydney said with anger in her voice.

"I already have a restraining order against him. Lot of good that did, huh?" Mimi's expression was one of sadness and distrust.

"Have you been to the hospital or to a doctor yet?" Sydney pulled back a bit trying not to stare.

"Too expensive. Not with working here and no medical insurance. That Edward Garrett is a cheap ...," she didn't finish her sentence before Antoine walked in. His face showed horror as Mimi turned to face him.

"What happened, honey?" he gasped without taking his coat off. Mimi held up her hands to keep him away. She knew he would try to hold her just as Sydney had. He stopped and directed her toward his tiny office down the hall for a little privacy. As she walked ahead of him, Antoine's wide eyes turned toward Sydney. She could see the horrifying questions he was asking her with his eyes.

Sydney slumped back onto the sofa and shook her head. What a monster. How could someone do that to another human being? What could have been the motivation for such a beating? She had obviously been down this road before. It was not the first time she had been the punching bag for this man.

Mimi came by a minute later, rewrapped in her coat, scarf and sunglasses. She waved a quick good-by and then hurried out the door. Antoine followed standing in lobby watching her leave.

"Unbelievable! I really hate that man. We'll just have to cover for her until she can put makeup on and heal a few of those bruises. She really needs the job." Antoine turned toward Sydney still shaking his head. "They picked up Amanda a few minutes ago for questioning." His voice was distressed and low. Continuing he added, "Terry is being held on robbery charges stemming from the purse incidents. I guess that's just so they don't have to free him just yet. If they do, they're afraid he'll run. He has no real home or anything to keep him here. There isn't anything substantial to tie him to the murder except his finger prints and of course, he was the last one to see him alive. But who knows. They can't really be sure there wasn't a motive on his part. So the robbery charges are just to keep him around is my guess." Antoine slumped on the sofa next to Sydney and buried his head in his hands. "This day has not started out very good. I don't know how I'm going to cope today. I'll be worried until Amanda gives me a call to say they let her go, and she's free. I don't know if that will happen though. The address change doesn't look good for her." Antoine sighed then added, "At least we know the real killer wasn't Mimi's husband. He wouldn't have used a little hand gun – he would have beaten Edward to death with his fists."

XVIII

Antoine called a small meeting before dance session was to start with Suzanna, Megan and Milli Mae Carter. Sydney guessed he would discuss Mimi and divide up her students between the two teachers. Both worked with new students as did Mimi.

Sydney was out on the dance floor with a dance chart trying to decipher a few new patterns in Waltz when Rick and Chandler arrived.

"Well, it's official," Chandler announced.

"Tell her the good news," Rick chided.

"Tonight I'll be doing the 'Splish splash' number in a towel," Chandler didn't look amused.

"What! Why did you agree to do that?" Sydney asked.

"Attention, obviously. I'll do anything to get attention," Chandler said flatly. Somehow, Sydney sensed that as much as he complained, he was actually looking forward to shocking everyone and getting a few laughs. That was just the way he was – laid back and easy going, yet ready willing and able to joke around with everything he did.

118

Chandler was the kind who used his humor growing up to avoid getting teased and bullied. He was never one of the "popular" kids, but was always doing or saying humorous things to get their attention. Otherwise no one would ever notice him. He would fade right into the background. If Chandler had killed Edward, Sydney thought, he would have bragged about it immediately with a bit of humor. But he really never even said a word about the murder or Edward – ever. It's as if he took no notice of him at all. They were just worlds apart.

The day went on as usual. Megan and Milli Mae showed both disgust at Mimi Clark's beating and an underlying excitement for more students and lesson time. They were paid only for the lessons they taught, so the name of the game was to fill up your schedule to maximum capacity. Now theirs would be full and their paychecks fatter.

Megan, good friend that she was, called Mimi immediately after the meeting and offered her small but quaint apartment for Mimi and her daughter. "We've got to keep you safe," she said. "Your mom's house is not safe anymore. Why don't you think about staying with me for a while?"

She listened to the answer on the other end of the phone. "I know the police are looking for him. That's why we have to get you out of there. Knowing you called the police will just make him madder then ever. Take a taxi over to my apartment. I'll take my lunch and meet you there with the keys. OK? Twenty minutes, and I'll be there."

She got off the phone. "Got to skip dance session today if that's OK. I need to take care of my friend." Antoine and Suzanna both nodded an understanding agreement.

"Be back in time for your first lesson," Antoine cautioned.

"Right. Chandler, can you drive me? Have you got your car today?" Megan grabbed her hat and purse.

Chandler just grinned and followed her out the door to the parking lot, glad that someone trusted him to drive them anywhere.

"Dance session!" Suzanna yelled to an almost empty room. When she realized how few teachers were left, she began to titter as if she had just made a joke.

"Hey, I've got some pictures we might want to use on the board over there. Everyone take a look at them and see if you see something interesting," Sydney said plopping the photos on the desk in front of Morgan Canfield. She hoped that someone might notice something out of the ordinary about those shows although she didn't know what that would be. Nothing seemed to be amiss.

Amanda called Antoine during the afternoon to say that she was no longer at the police station. Everything seemed to be fine although she had the feeling they still viewed her as a suspect. Plans for Edward's funeral were finalized. Amanda and Edward's first wife had joined forces to plan a religious service at the downtown church Edward had attended. That Edward belonged to a church surprised Sydney until Suzanna said something significant to explain.

"Eddie G. did everything 200%. It was all or nothing with him. So when he exercised, it was constant. When he dieted, it was seeds and water. When he did drugs, he was always high. And when he was into religion, it was whole heartedly. He never did anything half way. Whatever he was into, it consumed his entire life for that month or year or however long it lasted. He was a big ball of energy that plowed into something like a bowling ball rolls over the pins." Sydney had to agree. They both nodded as they thought it through. He was an unusual person that was certain.

At nine o'clock that evening as everyone was ready to head out to the floor for their last lesson of the day, Suzanna made a surprise announcement. "Important meeting right after last lessons tonight.

Everyone must attend." She didn't look upset, but rather in a pondering mood staring out the window as she spoke.

What could be so crucial that Suzanna would call a late night meeting? Sydney thought. Had they solved the case? Were they arresting Terry? Suzanna seemed to be calm without too much emotion. She wasn't worried or upset. What could this be about?

As everyone sat around the glass tables in the ballroom waiting for the meeting to begin, the night people began to meander by the door and peer through the curtained windows. There seemed to be more than usual. Maybe the news of the murder had created a stir – a media frenzy that called attention to the studio for spectators. Whatever the case, people seemed to wander by more than before and the darkness heightened the view from outside.

Suzanna stood before the group and began her speech: "I received an interesting letter today that is of utmost importance to all of us. It has to do with the regional testing of teachers. Those of you who have been here for a while know that the studios in this region require a yearly certification of all teachers. This year the testing is in Chicago. Edward of course knew of this event but failed to give me a heads up as to the date and arrangements. Thankfully, today a letter came with a reminder that stated all of the particulars. I'm sure the original information is sitting on Edward's desk in his office, which is sealed off as you know. The date is coming up quickly – a week from Friday to be exact. For those of you who are unaware of what this entails, let me explain. We travel to Chicago by car after our last lesson on Friday. The testing begins Saturday morning at nine o'clock. Each of you will be tested in the area of your expertise. Those who work with new students will be tested as Specialists, advanced teachers as Teachers, Antoine as the new student Counselor and myself as the Supervisor of the advanced department. The testing includes a written test, dance test, teaching test, and simulations of problem situations. It is quite grueling I can promise you. There is more than certification at stake here. There will be three groups formed from the top scoring individuals. Gold, Silver and Bronze. Each group will consist of three Specialists, five Teachers, one Counselor, and one Supervisor. I need not tell you that those who make these teams are recognized nationally by the organization as well as receiving honor locally. So this is quite an important career event."

Everyone sat quietly taking in the information. Those who had experienced the testing before simply nodded their heads in agreement with Suzanna's assessments.

She continued. "As you all know, Edward is a showman. He always took great pride in his teachers and his studio's dance standards. So he as usual offered us as the evening show after the testing is concluded. That means we have about a week and a half to get a dance number together for performance. Last year we did the Hustle that you all performed at Frankie's the other evening. So it can't very well be that routine, and it must involve the entire staff. Although Edward rarely took my choreography very seriously, I take this opportunity as a personal challenge to showcase my abilities as a choreographer. And I would appreciate any support from all of you as I put together a spectacular routine worthy of this event. It would benefit your careers as dancers and mine as a director. Could we all work together on this endeavor to give a great effort through this time of studio hardship? It would mean very much to me if you all would agree to give an extra effort as well as extra time. Is that possible for all of you? We will work on test preparation during our dance sessions and meetings this week and next if you all will come in early and stay late for rehearsals." Suzanna awaited a response from the group.

They all looked around at each other. Of course what could they say? They all knew it would benefit everyone if they agreed. "Of course," Antoine answered for the group.

"I expected more grumbling and complaining," Suzanna laughed obviously relieved with the response.

"We'll grumble and complain next week after all the extra rehearsals and less sleep," Chandler commented. Everyone laughed.

"Then go home. Get some sleep. I'll have a piece of music and some choreography for you tomorrow morning. We'll meet at ten and rehearse for about two or three hours before dance session. Megan," she turned to the smiling woman, "could you work on costumes after we decide on the music and theme?"

There was nothing that Megan liked better than to shop for costume ideas. "I'll use my lunch hours for that," Megan volunteered with a delighted grin.

"I'll make a list of partners for tomorrow. Let's have a great week and a half of preparation," Suzanna said in closing. "Don't forget what your motivation is – this studio and all of the teachers remaining."

XIX

Everyone was in attendance. Everyone that is except Craig Fritz.
Had anyone called him about this rehearsal? Sydney stood by the notice
in the back room and read the partner assignments. She was paired with
Craig.

"Sorry," Suzanna apologized as she tacked the paper to the
board. "It's just that you are so reliable – always at practice and on time.
You remember your routines so well that I knew you could handle Craig
and his no show attitude."

Sydney nodded in agreement. It wasn't like it would be too bad.
Craig was a good dancer and a great partner – that is if he could learn the
routine. Besides, Sydney had the feeling that Craig was somehow the
link to the Edward Garrett murder puzzle. She was sure he knew
something he wasn't telling. Otherwise why had he given her the strange
description of Tom Potter. It was an intentional lie she knew. He had to
have some reason other than a simple joke. It was certainly not that.

Today Craig Fritz was there for practice. Late, but he was there.
Suzanna was in the corner chatting away with him as everyone else
ambled unto the floor. The ballroom, usually scattered with exercisers at
this early morning hour, was now empty except for the studio teachers

dressed in grubbies. Amanda Garrett was at the church making funeral arrangements for Edward, so exercise class had been cancelled for the week. That left the floor wide open for their much needed practice.

Craig was putting on a piece of music. Suzanna with her eyes closed was swaying to the beat. He put on another song, and again she began to sway.

"Second one," Craig said. Suzanna nodded in agreement.

"OK people. Let's get started." Suzanna listened again to the start of the second piece – a new disco number that was currently beginning to get some radio air time. It was a patriotic song to an updated disco beat.

"This definitely calls for something red, white and blue," Megan was saying to Suzanna as she bopped her head to the rhythm. Suzanna nodded in agreement. "I'll get on it today," Megan added.

Suzanna outlined her entrance and lined up the couples. Her choreography while not as elaborate as Edward's was clearly well thought out and involved more lifts and showier lines. Edward tended to select movements that he himself could easily do. He didn't like to actually challenge himself with more than he was capable of doing.

Suzanna did not have those limitations, and her moves would definitely take some practice time.

The practices that week went well. Except of course when Rick Krist slid Megan through his legs during one of the new drop moves and let go of her hands. She careened across the dance floor on her back with her skirt up around her head. She was not hurt except for a few slivers she claimed lodged in her pantyhose. However she did not speak to Rick for the rest of the day until he brought her a box of candy as a peace offering. Nerves were occasionally frayed but on the whole everyone seemed focused.

Craig Fritz was not always there but choosing the music had given him some ownership to the routine. So he tried to make the early morning rehearsals as often as possible and was always around for the late practices. He usually talked someone into going out afterwards for a few dances at Frankie's.

The dance sessions went over basic teaching and dance techniques that they would need for the testing, and the meetings covered the oral and written tests. Sydney felt fairly prepared by the time Friday rolled around.

In the midst of rehearsals and meetings and teaching lessons was Edward Garrett's funeral. The church was downtown, so the teachers walked over together in the middle of the day. The studio was closed down for a few hours. There were quite a few mourners gathered when they entered so they sat fairly close to the back of the church.

Sydney tried to pay close attention to people she didn't recognize. Scanning the people ahead of her, she noticed Edward's first wife sitting with Amanda. His son of about ten years old sat between them. Edward's parents sat in front of the two wives. They were both getting up in age. Although Edward rarely mentioned his parents, Sydney had heard they were estranged and had been for many years. They lived out of state and had never been to the studio while she was there. A few of Amanda's model friends clumped together a few rows behind the family.

A high school friend that Edward remained close to was also in attendance. Sydney couldn't remember his name – was it Godfrey or something like that? He seemed to hang around Edward or rather mooch off of Edward whenever he was in town. Godfrey seemed to be a loser. But Edward had stayed in contact with him for some reason. Maybe it gave him a superior feeling to have someone to order around in spite of

Godfrey's needy nature. Or maybe Godfrey was blackmailing Edward. They had known each other since childhood. Maybe he had something he held over Edward's head. No, Godfrey seemed too dumb to do something like that. Whenever Sydney spoke to him or listened in on any conversation he was having, he didn't seem to have any intelligence whatsoever. Godfrey seemed genuinely distraught over the funeral. He hung his head and hunched over in his seat – probably thinking he no longer had his friend Edward to hang onto. Edward's women friends no doubt were appealing to a balding, chubby middle-aged man who had never married nor seemed capable of meeting anyone on his own. A sad situation to be sure.

The closed casket was surrounded by framed photos of Edward as well as several bouquets of bright colorful flowers. Amanda had carefully chosen special music from Edward's personal collection. His music collection was incredible and probably worth quite a bit if sold. They all filed one by one past this homage shaking hands with Amanda and the other family members who formed the greeting line. The air hung heavy and somber, but life went on.

The early morning rehearsal on Friday was a dress rehearsal, so Megan had brought in her costumes and was busy fitting everyone. The patriotic theme of the music offered her a unique choice. The women wore red leotards with white and blue stripes around the square necklines. The body suit was unique in that it did not cut up the leg in the French cut that Edward always preferred for his dancers. Instead the legs were cut in a little boy style – short shorts. The leo was then wrapped with an ankle length red skirt that clung slightly when the dancer stood perfectly still yet twirled out when in a spin. Finally, each dancer wore a red, white and blue head band wrapped around the entire head for those with short hair and tied around the top knotted pony tail for those with longer hair. It looked very different than anything they had ever worn before. Megan stood back with a smile of pride as the group starred into the mirror for final approval.

"I think it looks good," she nodded.

Suzanna agreed. "It's different. Unique." She stood back and gave an approving look. The men wore black pants and white billowing silk shirts with a red, white and blue tie knotted down at the middle of the chest so the shirt could unbutton a little at the top. The look was one that definitely went with the music and the movements.

Craig came in carrying his black pants at the very end of the rehearsal. So much for a "dress rehearsal", Sydney thought as he walked by without an apology. He grabbed his white shirt to try on.

"Do you have a few minutes to rehearse before meeting?" he asked as he headed toward the restroom.

Sydney was steamed. "I've been rehearsing since 9:30," she announced through a seething glare. "You'll have to do better than a minute before meeting."

"OK, OK. Do you have an hour free this afternoon?" Craig shot back before disappearing down the hall. He didn't even wait for her response.

At 10 o'clock that night the packed bags and costumes were piled in the corner by the back door. They would take several cars for the long drive to Chicago. That meant driving all night to get there by the 9:00 start of the test.

Suzanna divided the group up, and they began to load the cars that were parked in the lot near the pay window. "Make sure you switch off drivers so you aren't too tired for testing," she warned. "Please sleep in the car," she added with a pleading tone to her voice. They all just smiled back.

132

Sydney was in Edward's older Cadillac with Craig Fritz, Milli Mae Carter, and Chandler Dane. Craig was going to drive the first leg, and then Chandler would take over half way there. Milli Mae didn't have a driver's license, and Sydney avoided driving at all costs. She was in the city after all with plenty of bus transportation.

Chandler was still reeling from his party routine preformed that evening with Megan. Megan had begun the routine calmly as if doing a fun little 50's routine. She had on a poodle skirt and saddle shoes. She twisted across the floor with a pouty little expression on her face doing a few dance steps by herself. Suddenly, Chandler poked his head out from the kitchen door – his hair dripping a bit with water. Then he opened the door fully, revealing his tall skinny body wrapped in a towel. The crowd gasped and then began to laugh after the shock wore off. Chandler was scrubbing his back with a toilet bowl brush. That almost sent the audience into fits. The music was hardly audible over the noises from the crowd. Somehow they made it through the routine actually dancing together. Megan was grinning from ear to ear as she stood to accept her just applause. Chandler's face was beet red as he took a bow and then rushed back to the kitchen for his clothes. The audience didn't move. They had laughed so hard, they didn't even feel like standing up to dance a little themselves. The last dance was over before anyone actually got out onto the floor. It had been a memorable night. Luckily some of the staff had brought their own cameras for a few choice shots of the performance.

Craig started the car and pulled out into the city street. Milli Mae and Chandler stretched out in the back seat, and Sydney promptly fell asleep in the front before they even got out of town. It was a straight shot along the highway – a boring ride in the dark through small towns and farm land. There would be little traffic on a Friday night heading east at this time of year.

Craig had the radio playing some funky tunes, but Sydney didn't hear any of it. She was too tired from all the extra rehearsals that week. Suddenly she felt a hand shake her awake. Prying her eyelids open, she felt a strange stillness. The car was stopped. The dark night was split with light. It was the flashing of a police car.

A face was peering in through the window on Craig's side. "Excuse me," the voice was saying. "You'll have to follow me into town to the city hall."

"What's going on?" Chandler was just waking in the back seat.

"I guess I was going a little too fast," Craig was saying. "We have to go into town to pay the fine. They only take cash. How much do you all have?"

"What?" That woke Milli Mae up. "You did what? And now you expect us to pay up? You've got to be kidding."

"It's either that or jail for all of us. Do you want to make it to the testing on time or not? This little delay will cost us time." Craig was rather matter of fact about the whole situation. The rest of the group began to dig into pockets and purses as he followed the squad car off the highway.

They sat in front of the building marked City Hall pooling money and grumbling. Craig collected the fine and went in to settle.

"That's it," Chandler was saying. "I'm driving. No more of this crap." He got out of the car and positioned himself in the driver's seat.

"We all voted, and I'm driving the rest of the way," he growled as Craig tried to climb back into his former seat. Craig shrugged his shoulders and climbed in the back seat with Milli Mae. Without another word, he dozed off. Chandler just shook his head in disgust.

They made it to Chicago at 8:30 – a half an hour before the test was to begin. Parking the car and dragging out their bags, the four of them were met by a frantic Suzanna. "Where have you been?" she demanded.

"It's a long and expensive story," Chandler remarked passing her to find his room.

"We'll tell you later," Sydney groaned. "We don't have much time to change and slug some coffee before the start of the test." Suzanna just nodded and let them pass.

Sydney entered the hotel ballroom with the teachers from about eight of the other Midwestern states. The place was filled. Women trying to look their best, wore dressy cocktail dresses and heels even at 9:00 in the morning. Sydney wore a plain beige dress and her dance shoes. She had managed to tie her hair up and put some make up on. She hoped the bags under her eyes weren't too evident.

They divided everyone into four groups – Specialists, Teachers, Counselors, and Supervisors. The room was sectioned off into testing areas with the help of dividers. Each person was given their own schedule and a map. Sydney started in the oral teaching area. She was to teach a pretend student a specific dance pattern. Then she moved on to the written exam.

By the end of the afternoon, she felt a weariness setting in. Her head hurt, her feet hurt, and her bones hurt. She desperately wanted sleep. But it was only forty five minutes until the banquet was to begin. They would announce the three regional teams before the food was served. Then the banquet and finally their performance to start the evening dance. It was so rare that teachers were able to just dance with each other in a social setting that this would be a welcome event for most. They usually were trying to service students at a dance such as this. It might be fun, she thought.

She hurried to the room she was sharing with Megan, Milli Mae, and Anna Smith. The room was already a total mess – clothing scattered everywhere, make up on top of every possible piece of furniture, and suitcases flung open across the floor making walking totally impossible.

"Don't break your neck," Anna called out as Sydney stood in the doorway trying to navigate a route to the bathroom. "Megan already nabbed the shower," Anna informed her. "And remember to carry your costume down to dinner. We won't have time to come back up in between."

The men were divided into two rooms on either side of them. Carson, Richard and Antoine were in one, and Craig, Rick, and Chandler in the other. Suzanna was with Morgan and Darian Gray across the hall. Darian had flown in just for the banquet and would fly out right away in the morning. The rest would stay for additional training and a dance session until mid afternoon on Sunday.

"Let's fly!" Milli Mae was pressing the others to hurry. She had already spiked up her short bleached blond hair, donned a new coat of make up and a slinky silver dress. "I've got my eye on one of those Ohio boys," she added. She grinned at Megan who rolled her eyes and put the finishing touch on her bright red lips.

Sydney was wearing a silky red pants suit and was pulling her costume together to carry down to the banquet room. Her feet were killing her.

Anna shook out her curly hair and tied the costume scarf tightly around her head. She was wearing a white full skirt and shirtwaist style top that hung loose over a navy blue shell.

They got down to the newly transformed ballroom right on time. The partitions were gone and the round banquet tables with white linen table cloths circled the dance floor. Centerpieces of dried flowers elegantly decorated each table. A podium and head table stretched across the north end of the floor. Soft music was beckoning the dancers to enter, mingle, and enjoy a cocktail.

"Before we begin our evening meal," the announcer was motioning for the music to end. He waited a moment until every head turned toward the podium. "We will announce the three teams of top scoring dancers." He gave a great speech about how well everyone had done and how much it means to place on these teams. Teachers circled the dance floor eagerly awaiting the announcement.

"We will begin with the third place team consisting of three Specialists, five Teachers, a Counselor, and a Supervisor." Sydney held her breath. Could she possibly make it on the third place team? She hoped so. Richard Gray was one of the Specialists, and Suzanna was the Supervisor. Everyone clapped as they received their awards. Then another inhale of air as they awaited the second team announcement. Anna Smith was one of the Teachers on the second team along with Megan as number one Specialist and Antoine as Counselor. Anna and Antoine grabbed each other on the way up to the front, jumping up and down excitedly.

That's it, thought Sydney. I didn't even place on any of the teams. Oh, well, neither did Craig, and he's been around forever. She hung her head.

"For our first team...," they announced the Specialists first. "For our teachers, in fifth place, Carson Hunter." The studio clamored around Carson as he tried to make his way through the crowd to the front. "Fourth place, Shelly Nelson. Third place, Daniel Madison. Second place, Sydney Monroe. And in first place, Marilee Graham. Come up to receive your awards."

"Sydney! Go up and get your award," someone was calling in her ear. "Sydney!" Sydney didn't quite hear what was being said to her. She walked in a daze up to the front unable to believe that they had actually called her name. And on the first team too.

The rest of the studio teachers were screaming madly as she took her award and made her way back to the table. Rick Krist was opening a bottle of champagne and pouring her a glass. She downed it, and he filled it again. Wow, this was exciting. Second place. Unbelievable!

Suzanna Caldwell sat down next to Sydney. "Congrats on a job well done." She tipped her glass toward Sydney's. Suzanna looked like a silent movie star tonight. She had her contacts in making her eyes seem huge and heavy lidded. Her sleek bobbed hair was pulled back away from her tiny face and her make up heavier than her daily look. She wore a slinky cocktail dress in a glittery copper tone with a matching hand bag.

Pulling a long slim cigarette from her bag, she lit up blowing the smoke out of the side of her mouth. She laughed heartily as she leaned back in her chair.

"So what will you do now that Edward is gone?" Sydney asked as she watched Suzanna take a drag on her cigarette.

"Well, obviously Amanda is the new owner. I don't know what will change if anything. Maybe she'll even sell the place for all I know." Suzanna leaned a bit forward. "It certainly puts me in the clear as far as suspects."

Sydney looked at her questioningly.

Suzanna laughed. "It would have been a weapon of choice for me – I mean a small pistol is certainly something I would use. And there were enough reasons for me to want him dead. But I would have waited just a little longer until Edward and Amanda finally got a divorce. Then I might have had a chance of being the benefactor or at least part owner of the studio. That would have been more to my advantage." She laughed again and lifted her champagne glass for a refill.

It took a while for the meal to come. Their table happily downed more champagne in celebration, so they didn't seem to notice that they would be served last. Sydney could feel her eyelids drooping. The excitement, the champagne and no sleep hadn't improved her physical exhaustion. Coupled with no food until now, she was slowly slumping in her chair as her plate of banquet chicken and rice was placed in front of her.

After the meal, Suzanna was urging the group to begin changing into their dance costumes. Sydney rose and felt a wave of nausea. The room seemed to be spinning. She carefully held on to her chair and then reached over to Craig. He took her arm and walked with her to the cluster of restrooms in the hallway.

"Need a hand at changing?" he asked with a leer.

"No. But I don't know how I'm going to do this routine. Everything seems fuzzy," Sydney said slowly holding her forehead.

"Don't worry. You can count on me," he said with a rare tone of sincerity.

"You'll have to help me," she pleaded.

"Your feet won't even touch the floor."

And they didn't. Somehow when the music began and the group in their bright red dresses danced out onto the floor, Sydney's feet didn't even touch the floor. Craig lifted her up off the ground on every movement and correctly remembered every step. In the final pose, he lifted her up to his shoulders and carried her majestically off the floor as the crowd clapped wildly.

XX.

In spite of her hazy state, Sydney thoroughly enjoyed her evening. She began to sober up once the routine was over and she no longer swilled the glasses of champagne that Rick Krist was pouring for the others. Dancing with the other teachers was a pleasure. They didn't talk about studio business or death or Terry Crawford. It was a welcome change from the past week.

Sydney had kept her costume on. It was too much trouble to change back and forth. In spite of her earlier exhaustion, she felt a wave of energy that carried her through to the last dance of the evening.

Milli Mae had indeed snagged an Ohio boy – a dark haired cutie who was only about two inches taller than she was. Suzanna had long ago gone to her room with Morgan. Morgan, not a dancer, had found the whole evening quite boring. Her complaining for the first hour had driven many to other tables or up on the dance floor whenever possible. Richard and Darian Gray had danced one dance and then left abruptly. Carson Hunter, ever the night owl, was still sitting in the same chair he had grabbed during dinner. Occasionally up for a dance, he had vegetated comfortably for most of the night. Rick Krist and Chandler had made their way around the room all evening, asking anyone who didn't seem attached to dance. Where they had gone now was anybody's guess. Megan Meeker had left half way through the evening to head to bed. Her usually vibrant smile had puckered. She lay her head down and found her eyes fluttering to a close early on.

Sydney ambled back to the room still basking in the awards of the evening. She found herself breaking into a smile for no apparent reason as she slowly wandered the halls of the hotel. Turning the corner toward their hallway, she spotted Craig sitting in the stair well.

"Thanks for saving my butt tonight," she gratefully acknowledged. Her voice was soft and a little grating from all of the shouting and liquor.

Craig looked up. He nodded and dropped his chin into his hands. "No problem."

"What? No beautiful lady on your arm tonight?" Sydney pretended to look around peering into the corners.

He chuckled slightly.

"I expected you to ask me to accompany you to your room. Where's the pick up line?"

"Don't tell anyone. I wouldn't want my reputation to get tarnished," he mumbled.

"You're way too quiet. What's wrong with you?" Sydney didn't know how to respond to a subdued Craig. She was used to his bragging and swagger. This was hard to take.

"It may surprise you, but I happen to be in love. With someone I can't have," he confided. "Don't tell anyone please. I did you a favor. Now I have to trust that you keep this secret."

"What's wrong with being in love?" Sydney asked with a menacing shrug.

"It's something for everyone else, but not Craig Fritz. I have a reputation to live up to, you know." He didn't seem to know what to do with the situation. He seemed a broken and frustrated man. His long thin face seemed more hollow than usual, and he didn't meet her eye to eye.

"It's been a long day that's all," she ventured. "Tomorrow everything will feel different. You'll see." She almost wanted to put her arm around her shoulder but that would be like a sheep trying to comfort the poor sad wolf with a tear in his eye. You never knew if it was real or a ploy to pounce. "Well, good night." She hastily retreated to her room and crawled into bed for a much needed night of sleep.

The dance session began slowly with teachers wandering into the huge ballroom at will usually carrying a large cup of hot coffee. Some were content to simply sit down at one of the back tables and watch the whole thing. Nationally known judge and dancer Clyde Sullivan was patiently at the front of the room demonstrating some of his critically acclaimed dance patterns. Those who joined in were impressed and delighted with some new and different moves.

Sydney was there from the start – of course. Ever on time it would have been an irritation to walk in late. Carson and Megan were also there fairly early on in the session. Milli Mae and Craig never made it down. Suzanna and Antoine came in early on with Richard Gray. Darian was scheduled to fly out earlier that morning. Chandler and Rick straggled in at the very end. Rick had on sunglasses in spite of being indoors.

After lunch was served buffet style in the back of the ballroom, Suzanna arranged the rides home. Some opted to leave early and not attend the afternoon session. Sydney chose to stay so ended up in a car with Suzanna, Antoine, and Richard on the way back.

Hauling her suitcase out to Antoine's non-descript Camero, Sydney tossed it in the trunk and climbed in next to Richard who was already napping. Antoine settled into the driver's seat, adjusted his sunglasses and flashed a smile at Suzanna nestled in the bucket seat in the front. "Ready?" he chimed.

There was no answer so he put the car into gear and pulled away from the curb. Babbling a bit about who knows what, he was surprisingly animated after a tiring weekend.

Finally, Suzanna opened one eye and spoke. "So what do you think Amanda will do with the studio?"

"I don't think she's interested in the studio as much as she loves the chance to exercise in the mornings. Why? You interested in buying it?" Antoine's eyebrow lifted above the frame of his glasses.

"Maybe." There was a pause then she added, "Maybe, I'd be interested in being a part owner. You know I haven't saved up any nest egg working for Edward Garrett. I have a little, but maybe I could try to get a loan from relatives if someone else wanted to go in with me. You at all interested?"

"Actually, I hadn't even thought about it. It's an interesting idea." Antoine seemed to mull over the thought making a few hemming and hawing noises. Sydney closed her eyes as if asleep but remained closely tuned in to the whole conversation.

"Who else might be interested? Do you have any ideas? It would have to be someone I could trust to let the business run in the way it should without many changes in the system. We have it just the way it should be without someone coming in with some wild idea to change everything around. At least Amanda wouldn't do that I don't think," Suzanna guessed.

"No, I don't think Amanda is interested in making changes. She might even be interested in a quick sale if she thought she could keep the exercise class going. That's all she really cares about. She was never interested in the dancing – Edward kept her in there dancing because he loved it. It was never her." Antoine was now speeding along the highway, eyes fixed on the road.

"Let me think this through," Suzanna twisted her face into a thought provoking expression. "Hey, Sydney. Do you still have those photos from the club? I'd like to take another look at them."

Sydney sighed and turned over to grab her purse stuffed into the space between her feet and the seat in front of her. "Yeah. I haven't really looked them over too closely. If you see something, let me know." She handed the stack to Suzanna and snuggled back down into her seat.

Suzanna flipped through the glossy stack, occasionally giggling or snorting. "It's hard to believe he's not here," she finally sighed. "I guess it will hit me soon that he won't sail through that front door bellowing at someone about wearing the wrong colored suit or not wearing enough lipstick. I'll never really lose the feeling I first get when I enter the studio – that feeling of immediately cowering for fear of a flying ashtray. Actually, in spite of all the discomfort, I will miss him. I'll miss the surprise of a gold bracelet at Christmas and the occasional compliments that would take me through the next few weeks feeling up in the clouds. I'll miss the humor of his tirades and the look of shock on the face of a new teacher the first time they see him as he really is – was.

I'll miss the way he always checked his hair and the sudden grin of a wolf ready to pounce on a poor unsuspecting sheep every time a pretty young girl walked by. I'll miss watching his amazing ideas for routines and the excitement he had when finding a newly released tune that inspired an idea for a new dance. You could actually see the wheels in his head turning when that happened. It was pretty amazing. He's just a one of a kind."

Antoine nodded in agreement then suddenly slammed on his brakes. A willowy deer and her fawn crossed the road ahead. The wooded rural area was bathed in the pink glow of sunset, and the startled fawn stood frozen in the middle of the road wide eyed and staring at the car stopped a few feet in the distance then quickly scampered into a clump of dark firs that lined the road.

"Wow, that was lucky. Those things can really damage your car if you hit one," Suzanna gasped as she dropped the stack of pictures, pushed her glasses back up her nose, and clung to the car seat. "We're lucky there is so little traffic."

Richard groaned as he came to life. Shaking his head and sitting up into his usual straight as a board posture, he reached for the pictures that were scattered around his feet.

"Richard," Antoine laughed, "you're among the living again. You must not have stayed up too late last night. You and the wife left fairly early."

"Yeh, Darian wasn't feeling good, so we turned in early." He let out a sigh, put the pictures back into a stack, and sat staring at the top one. "When were these taken?"

"Half of them are the show right before Edward was killed, and the others are from the show you and I did afterwards," Sydney answered stretching forward to relieve her back ache. "I'm feeling surprisingly good today in spite of my over indulgence of champagne last night. It sure was fun though." She lay her head back and grinned.

Richard was clinging tightly to the pictures shuffling one at a time through each one. "That one of us is especially great, don't you think? It really captures that line exactly," Sydney pointed to the colorful glossy on the top of the pile.

Richard was silent. He just kept shuffling through over and over again. Finally, he put them into two piles and tried to arrange the order according to the routine sequence. His face was pale.

"You don't look very good," Sydney said staring into his face.

"I don't feel very well," he muttered.

"Maybe you've got what Darian has," Suzanna offered.

"I doubt that. She's got what they call pregnancy." He didn't actually smile. His mouth sort of formed a long straight line across his narrow face.

"Congratulations dad!" Antoine shouted.

Richard just nodded without saying anything more for the rest of the trip. Antoine dropped everyone off at their respective homes when they got back.

XXI.

Sydney was too tired to go into exercise class the next morning and besides it was Monday. When she got to the studio around 12:30 she expected the awards to be sitting on the front desk and a lot of enthusiastic noise about the weekend's success. There was noise all right, but it wasn't about the weekend. Suzanna Caldwell was at the desk with Morgan and Joan Ericson who hadn't joined the group for the testing. They were buzzing about something important.

"What's going on?" Sydney asked when no one seemed to pay any attention to her entrance in spite of the door clang that announced her presence.

"Latest news on the Edward Garrett murder," Suzanna began. "Richard Gray has confessed to the police that he is the killer."

"No way," Sydney shook her head. "There is no way that Richard killed Edward."

"That's what I said," Joan agreed. "This makes no sense at all. None whatsoever." She walked around to the back of the desk to check the appointment schedule for the day. "The police just called Morgan with the news. There has got to be some mistake."

An hour later when the group was assembled in the ballroom around the glass tables, two police detectives were standing nervously in front of them preparing to address the latest news.

"As you have already heard," the first began, "we have a suspect in the Edward Garrett murder. The case will officially close with this confession by Richard Gray. We believe him to be the killer of Garrett. You can all rest easy now that we have a conclusion to this case."

"What possible motive would Richard have for murdering Edward?" Joan questioned as the detective fidgeted with his jacket sleeve.

"Basically, he hated the guy," was the pronouncement.

""Not good enough!" Sydney retorted.

"Excuse me?" the detective frowned. He had obviously expected relief and not hostility from the dancers.

"Everyone hated the guy. That's no motive. Besides why would Richard go so long without saying a word and then suddenly confess? Makes no sense," Sydney continued.

"Guilt?" He stared at her and then let his eyes pass around to the faces of the others who were waiting for an explanation.

"Sorry, I don't buy it." Sydney usually didn't stick her neck out this far, but something inside didn't feel right about this whole situation.

"The evidence we are currently gathering supports Richard Gray's confession," the detective continued with a defiant look at Sydney who sat arms crossed and glaring right back at him. "Surveillance tapes from the parking ramp show his car entering just before the time of the murder and leaving right after. That seems proof enough right there. And he described the murder weapon."

Sydney got up and walked around to the front of the desk area. The rest looked at each other for reaction. Some nodded an agreement and other just frowned pondering this latest information.

Sydney snatched a piece of scratch paper from the desk and headed back to the teachers' office. Sitting at Suzanna's immaculately clean desk, she began to make a list. Tapping the pencil eraser on the top of the sheet she began to think back to what had happened prior to the confession. Something had happened this past weekend to make Richard Gray walk into the police station on a Sunday night after the testing and confess to a murder he didn't commit. What had happened? Whatever it was, with a new baby on the way, it would have to be something really significant. A new baby doesn't deserve a father in prison. Richard would certainly have considered that.

Antoine, Suzanna, Megan Meeker, and Joan gathered in the office. Sydney explained her theory – something had happened this weekend to make Richard step up and take the blame for a horrible crime he had nothing to do with. They all began to think. What was the link?

"Well, he and Darian left the dance very early. I think they only stayed for one dance and headed to bed," Suzanna began.

"He said Darian was sick," Antoine added.

"What about the ride down?" Sydney asked.

"They both flew. Airline discounts, you know," Suzanna explained.

"He slept almost the whole trip back," Sydney recalled. "But the photos seemed to shake him up a bit. He looked sick that last hour or two. I'm going to check with Ken at the ramp on the car situation. It would seem that the police would have noticed that connection way before this. Why did it take them so long to recognize his car in the ramp?"

"By the way," Suzanna said peering over her glasses, "Terry was charged with petty theft and is spending a few weeks in the work house. The detectives just filled me in on that new bit of info. What will we do when he comes back? Should we let him keep his job? I don't know, with Richard in jail we're really short male teachers. We may have to keep him on as much as I hate to do it. Now to decide what to do with Richard's lessons for today…all week… all year!"

Ken sat in his usual spot in the exit booth of the parking ramp. He worked during the day and checked out about the same time as the studio staff around eleven. Ken was pushing his mid thirties and despite his ability to speak with knowledge about almost any subject you threw at him, he still worked in the same parking garage job he had begun after high school. Everyone knew him, and he knew everyone.

Sydney asked him about the tapes. He stuck his scraggly mop of brown hair out of the booth window and pushed his taped glasses back up his nose. Yes, he admitted, he remembered giving the police the tapes from that night. No, he didn't know what they had found. They hadn't been very talkative to him about anything, and he had left before the murder took place. The automated payment system went into effect after midnight.

"Well, they have Richard Gray for the murder," Sydney informed him.

Ken frowned. "I remember Richard leaving that night as usual. It would seem odd for him to come back later. He's one of the few who drives every day you know. He lives quite far away from the downtown area because his wife works at the airport. They live out there so she can get to work more easily."

Most of the staff lived close to the downtown area and took the bus. Edward, of course, always drove his car in spite of living only one block from the studio. He pulled one of his many cars into a special spot reserved just for him right along side Ken's booth so he could watch it during the evening hours. And Joan drove because her hours were different than the teaching staff. Otherwise most teachers – even Antoine – rode the bus back and forth.

Ken leaned out further. "Richard always drove that little compact thing, but his wife drove a mid sized newer model. It was a real nice silver Pontiac. She sometimes would pull in at night later. I saw her car parked right over there around midnight some times." He pointed to a spot a couple spaces past Edward's. "I think she went in the back because it's better lit around here, and it's a little scary around that time downtown."

Sydney trudged off to get some lunch and get back in time for her evening lessons. She grabbed a salad and drink at the little deli around the corner. The owner didn't speak much English, but smiled broadly and nodded politely at her food selection.

It was a dreary day – the weather was drizzly and cloudy and the feelings she had inside were just as bleak. She walked back to the studio in a foggy mood, questions rolling around her head about what had transpired that day. Should she just let it go? Or should she figure out why Richard would confess to a murder this late in the game. He was so meticulous, he would have gone to the police the moment he fired the gun. It wasn't in his character to let it go so long. Why would he come forward now after just finding out he was to become a father? The news would warrant him hiding any connection to the murder. Did he know about the parking ramp tapes and figure it was just a matter of time before they came looking for him? Maybe.

Suzanna was ranting in the back room holding the booking sheets in one hand and a pencil in the other. "What are we going to do? Richard Gray was booked solid. We have no one who can pick up his students?"

Antoine, the head of the new student department was looking hassled and tired. It would be his responsibility to teach all those lessons if they couldn't juggle them to other teachers.

Rick Krist stood up and gave Suzanna a defiant look. "I think you have a solution right here in front of your face, and you just don't know it." He glared at her eyes through overhung blond eyebrows.

"What! What solution do I have?" Suzanna usually calm and quiet, was a raving mess. The past few weeks had hit her hard and she was at the end of her rope.

"Your answer is right here," Rick grabbed Chandler Dane's shoulder and hauled him to his feet. "Here's the man for you. Tall, handsome (he snickered slightly at this remark), and a great dancer. He's a star in the making if you'd just give him a chance."

Chandler looked a bit embarrassed, his face reddening slightly. But he squared his shoulders and gave her confident look. "Yeah!" was all he could manage to squeeze out.

"Chandler?" Suzanna and Antoine looked first at Chandler and then at each other. It was obviously a thought that had never occurred to either of them. Her eyes passed up and down Chandler's lean frame. He wore a textured sports jacket over pressed creased pants. The pale blue shirt brought out the color in his eyes and the tie was a clever pattern that immediately brought conversation. "We could try it, I suppose," she slowly nodded. Her face softened and she no longer seemed in knots. "It just might work. It just might work."

With the rest of the group focused on Chandler, Megan grabbed Sydney and dragged her out to the dance floor. The turmoil seemed to pass at least for the moment. "I need a guinea pig to try my group class on," she explained placing Sydney on her right side in front of the mirror. Together they began an easy line dance starting with the left foot. Left side together side, tap. Right side together side, tap. Left turn, turn, turn, tap. Right turn, turn, turn, tap. Forward walk, walk, walk, tap. Back step, step, step, tap. Promenade left walk, walk, walk, turn. Promenade right walk, walk, walk, turn. Flick right, left, right – kick. Flick left, right, left – kick. Start over.

"Excellent!" Megan beamed as the music blared in the background. "That'll work."

"Here let me lead you...in honor of Richard Gray." Megan quickly put Sydney into dance position and began to lead traveling Paulistas. The Paulista is a Brazilian Samba step that rotates the woman from side to side in a curtsey position as it travels down the floor. Richard Gray, normally very conservative and proper in his dance style, somehow transformed this step into a total carnival ride for his partner by lifting her up as he swung her. All the women teachers would beg Richard for few Paulistas, and occasionally he would oblige sending them into squeals of laughter. Megan couldn't swing a partner like Richard could, but she tried. Sydney laughed out loud at the attempt. It reminded her that despite Richard's prim manner, deep down he had a sense of humor. It was a pleasant memory.

XXII

Craig Fritz was energized today. No longer the melancholy aloof person from the Chicago trip, he came in sporting a gleaming smile and a kind word for everyone.

"Too weird," was all that Morgan said as he passed the front desk with a quick compliment about her appearance. Shaking her head she continued to switch appointments to Chandler's column, looking up

161

phone numbers, and making calls to inform students of the change. She was excellent at presenting a diplomatic reason for the changeover claiming it was "a temporary change due to a personal situation that had arisen for Mr. Gray." Morgan was very good. It helped that the police hadn't made any charges as of yet so details were not currently out in the news media.

Chandler Dane was nervous but putting in every effort to go over programs and learn techniques he would need to teach Richard's bevy of students. He and Antoine were in Antoine's tiny office with doors closed in preparation.

The fat warm drops of rain began to splash slowly at first and then turned to a steady rhythm against the large window panes that circled the dance floor. Several teachers ran in from dinner covering their heads with thin jackets if they had bothered to carry one along. "Who knew this was coming?" Morgan chided as they shook off leaving damp spots on the entry carpet.

Following the group a few minutes later, Megan entered with a gloating smile and an umbrella hat in bright stripes of red, blue, green and yellow. The dome sat perfectly on her head sheltering her and her clothes. Not only was she greeted with a burst of laughter from the milling teachers, but she had a box in her hand that she presented to Carson Hunter standing at the front desk.

"For me?" he asked with a curious frown. His tedious grey vest that the other teachers commonly referred to as his "uniform" was showing a few drops of rain along with a few lunch stains – probably from last week.

"I forgot your birthday," she answered as he opened the box to a matching umbrella hat. He opened his dome, placed the hat on his head and proceeded out the door for a trial run in the sprinkles that continued to fall. The group crowded around the window for a few minutes of laughter before gathering up wet belongings to hang in the back teachers' office out of sight from the soon to arrive evening students.

A group class by Megan Meeker was something to behold. Sydney tried to keep an eye on her as she taught her own advanced group. Megan would capture everyone's attention with her wide bright red mouth. Whether smiling or talking about her chosen dance, she was always the center of attention. Tonight she had just demonstrated a pattern incorrectly. Boldly she declared, "I lied! I lied! I'm sorry, it should look like this. Here, come here, you, and let me try that again." She grabbed her demonstration partner — a bewildered student who once again showed the rest of the group the way to do the dance in a partner position instead of the solo line they had been doing. The group clapped wildly and began to try the new technique. The music pounded and the chatter of the students generated a mild din of excitement.

Sydney finished her group and spotted Craig lazily sprawled out on a chair watching the action on the floor. Never one to sit for long, his long legs stretched out in front of him as he hunched over in dreadful slumping posture. Edward Garrett had always said that Craig would be an excellent dancer if it weren't for his terrible posture.

"Hey, what's laughing boy doing on the floor? Did they finally give him a few students, or what?" he motioned to Chandler Dane who was cheerfully dancing around the floor with a young slender woman.

"They turned over Richard's students to Chandler now that he's in jail," Sydney whispered so no one else could hear.

"What! Why's Gray in jail?" Craig snapped to an erect posture.

"Quiet!" Sydney commanded with a snarling whisper. She positioned herself between Craig and the floor of milling students. "He confessed to Edward's murder. I have no clue why he would do that now, even if he did do it. He just found out he's going to become a new papa. Not the time to go running to the police for a confession if you ask me."

Craig's eyes narrowed to even beadier slits that usual. "Gray confessed to murder? Crazy! What's this stuff about becoming a 'papa'?"

"He found out in Chicago that Darian is pregnant. He seemed quite happy about it, then wham, he goes to the police and confesses to being a killer. Doesn't make sense to me," Sydney said with a shake of her head. "I'd be quiet about this for now. The students don't know anything about it."

Craig slowly got up out of the chair and without so much as another word made a path toward the back teachers' office. His earlier smile was now twisting into a scowl.

Sydney shrugged and shook her head before congratulating Megan on another superb group class. Chandler was just finishing with his student and heading out to the lobby to meet his next one. He flashed a tired but content smile at the two of them as he passed.

"I'm glad he's finally getting his chance," Sydney commented as he returned to the floor with a short stout woman with a bowl haircut. Her mouth was plastered with an admiring smile at her new teacher —

her head tilted back in an uncomfortable position in order to gaze up at his face towering above her.

"I'd love to chat, but gotta go," Megan waved and smiled at her student pacing back and forth next to the dance floor. "Mr. Beagan, how has your day been?" And she was off.

Sydney had a free hour. Her couple had called at the last minute due to a babysitting problem. She pulled the cancellation notice from the front spindle with a guttural growl. "Rescheduled for tomorrow," Morgan said without even looking up from her writing.

"Thanks," Sydney didn't really mind. With all that was going on lately, it was a nice break to just sit back and observe. The floor was filled with dancers. It didn't matter that the music playing was a Rumba. Everyone was doing their own dance. Sooner or later their music would come up, and they would scurry to the middle of the floor to work on the mechanics with the timing. It was a marvelous system. Everyone was happy, smiling and chatting as they moved around the room. You would hardly even know that this studio had been the scene of a brutal murder just a short time ago. It all seemed so normal tonight.

Sydney wandered back to the teachers' office to file her lesson book. Craig was huddled in the corner white and pale.

"Don't you feel well?" Sydney asked. He just made a grunting sound back. "You were so…what's the word? Peppy before. Just an observation that's all."

He moaned and buried his head in his large boney hands. His slender fingers covered his eyes and his long dark hair drooped over his forehead in oily ringlets. "This day started out so great …so great," was all he would say.

Sydney found Antoine in the hall and cornered him. "How's Chandler doing?"

"So far, so good. He's actually doing a fair job – not what I expected I'll admit. But he is a personality and knows basically how to dance. So we'll see," Antoine answered back with a half hearted nod.

"I have something to discuss with you," Sydney looked around to make sure no one was near. "Remember when I told you I'd keep my eyes open about Edward's murder? Well, when I told Craig about Richard's confession, he about lost it."

Antoine's left eyebrow lifted curiously. He turned to hear more.

"Richard and Craig are not that close. Why would it upset Craig so much that Richard confessed to murdering Edward? He wasn't very emotional about the murder in the first place. It makes no sense,"

Sydney told him about her conversation with Craig out on the dance floor and again her encounter with him in the teachers' office.

"I'll agree, it's very strange. I sort of forgot about the whole murder thing when Richard confessed. I thought that was it – it was all over now, and Amanda would be free from guilt. But now that you mention Craig's reaction, I don't think the situation is over at all..." Antoine wanted to continue but just at that moment, Chandler and his student appeared around the corner for a little chat. "Got to go," he whispered and scooted down the hall to show them into his tiny office space.

Just as the night was beginning to wind down and the students were on their way out the door, a detective showed up. He greeted the students' curious stares with a friendly nod and a tap to his hat but quickly turned his back to them and gathered the teachers together for a meeting in the reception area. A few students pressed their noses to the glass to get a glimpse of what was happening from the outside. The detective turned his face to stare out and motion them on their way before beginning his speech.

"As you know, we have Richard Gray in custody for the murder of Edward Garrett. He came to us and gave us a statement of confession.

168

Although there are some facts to support his claims, there are enough questions to make us keep an opened mind. Several of his explanations just don't add up. We have questions. Now we have a development that needs some help from you. We have a missing person. Darian Cooper Gray has disappeared. We have been checking with the airlines to see if she might have been called in for a flight, and we've checked to see if she might be visiting relatives with the confession of her husband causing her concern I'm sure. So far we have no word on either of these possibilities. We need your help in locating her. We need to be assured that she is in no danger and has not been a victim of foul play. Do any of you know where she might be?" The detective clasped his hands in front of him and glanced from face to face for any sign of reaction.

"Well, Craig, here...," Sydney turned to find Craig in the group but he was no where to be found.

"Yes, Miss...," the officer waited for her to fill in with "Monroe". "You were saying something about Craig?"

"It's just when I mention the news about Richard's confession to Craig Fritz earlier today, he suddenly became quite upset. I don't know if it has anything at all to do with Darian, but Craig is not one who has been very close to Richard Gray. It seemed strange, that's all." Sydney

169

tried to put her finger on what she was feeling. Her impression was that something about the whole situation was troubling to Craig for some reason, and that reason didn't quite make sense given the connections.

"I see," the officer wrote a few notes in a small notebook and then turned to the others for anything else.

"Richard said that Darian was pregnant," Suzanna ventured in case that was not something previously known.

The office stopped and stared at Suzanna intently. She continued, "He told us about it on our trip back from Chicago this past weekend."

He scratched his head. "Hmmm." It was evident he wanted to say more, but didn't. Maybe the police didn't know that little detail. The whole staff at the studio seemed well aware of it just nodding as Suzanna spoke.

"If anyone does hear from Darian, please call me right away," he placed a card with his name and number on the top of the reception desk. "Please, it's very important."

No one had bothered to turn off the music in the ballroom before the meeting, and a slow Bolero was playing quietly in the background as they watched the detective disappear out the front door. There was a stillness as the group began to gather up their belongings to head home.

Sydney decided it was time to look again at those photos from Frankie's. Richard Gray has suddenly changed his disposition after picking up the stack on the car ride home from Chicago. Something was in one of those photos. She carefully grabbed the stack from the drawer of her cubby and put them in her purse.

At home, she sat down on the floor to spread out the photos. She once again divided them into two piles – the before death and the after death. The after photos were fairly clear cut. With the attention on her and her dance partner, she had always paid a bit more attention to these. She could recall every detail because it was personal, but the photos from before bothered her. She hadn't actually been at Frankie's that night so she had nothing to go on. She spread those out and stared.

Something seemed amiss. The stacks of photos had been even before when she had divided them in the car to give to Suzanna. Now the before stack was smaller.

She grabbed the phone and dialed Suzanna's number.

"I know it's late," she began when Suzanna answered. There was a bit of chatter from the other end then Sydney continued. "Did you take out any of the Frankie photos to put up on the board?"

"No? Do you recall anything about those photos that seemed out of place?" Sydney had a gut feeling that there was something she should have noticed.

"OK. So who exactly was in those photos besides the dancers, Amanda and Edward?" She knew the Garretts were a certainty. There was nothing unusual about the photos of their routine. It had to be the others – the ones of the patrons in the background.

She grabbed a pen and began to write down names as Suzanna could recall. "Was Craig there?" she asked. Craig was always there. Frankie's was his hangout. "Thanks."

She hung up the phone and stared at the list. There must be a connection somewhere. Edward, Amanda, Antoine Hawks, Terry Crawford, Rick Krist, Chandler Dane, Milli Mae Carter, and Darian Gray. OK. Who was missing? Joan never went to Frankie's. Mimi only went when she danced. Megan was odd. She was usually there. And Craig. That was even odder. Strange that Richard wasn't in the picture if Darian was there. They were always there together. Anna wasn't

172

there of course, and Morgan the non-dancer never went to Frankie's. Suzanna didn't go that night either. That wasn't out of the ordinary. She recalled a photo of Antoine and Amanda chatting in the corner. Not too unusual. They were good friends. That picture wasn't in the stack.

She carefully went over the photos that remained. There was a picture of Chandler and Rick holding up their drinks, and one of Terry scowling at the dancers from the side of the floor. There had been one of Milli Mae draping her arms around Antoine's neck that was missing. Strange, but all of the photos of Antoine, Milli Mae and Darian were gone. Had there been one of Darian? She could recall seeing one before. Terry, Rick and Chandler were in a few more. What was the pattern here and who had taken the missing pictures? She had shoved them in her drawer after returning from Chicago. Someone would have had to go digging a bit to find them. Unless they were taken before she put them away. That would leave Richard, Suzanna, and Antoine who could have slipped a few out during the trip home.

Sydney couldn't sleep. She tossed and turned all night thinking about Amanda, the Grays, the missing photos, and the elusive Craig Fritz. Finally, at six in the morning she got up and walked down to the corner shop for a cup of fresh brewed coffee. She'd never actually been up this early before that she could recall and marveled at the clear air, the coo of the morning doves and the glow of the sunrise across the sky. Sitting on the park bench across the street from her apartment, she began to go over and over in her mind what had happened since Edward's death. She had always had a strange feeling that Craig was the key to the whole situation, and that feeling still nagged at her insides as she sipped her hot coffee.

Well, if she was going to do anything about this she would have to find Craig. And to find Craig, she would need a car.

At seven o'clock she returned to her apartment and rang Antoine. "Antoine? You up yet?" she didn't even bother to consider that this was an ungodly hour to a late night dancer.

"Who is this?" came the voice on the other end of the phone.

"It's Sydney."

"What time is it?" Antoine yawned loudly.

"Never mind. I have a plan, and I need you and your car." She went on to explain her plan. "You might as well pick up Megan on your way over here. I think we need a few people on this little trip."

An hour later, Sydney, Megan and Antoine were on their way to the suburbs. Traffic was still heavy in some parts, but as they turned on to a short residential street backing up to a small neighborhood park, there was not a person nor a car in sight.

They parked in front of a small cracker box – one story with a door in the middle and a shuttered window on each side. The driveway meandered back to a small one car garage tucked away behind the house. The owner Cutie Wilson was a former student and former part-time receptionist at the studio. She had a name that was perfect for an eight year old, dressed like a fifteen year old, and sagged older than the forty five she actually was. Cutie lived here with her nineteen year old son and her twenty year old boyfriend. She was also Craig Fritz's landlady. Craig rented a small bedroom in the back of the house.

They knocked on the door. No one answered. They knocked again. This time Cutie opened the door. She wore a short wrapped robe made from a shiny patterned silk. Cutie was short and compact. If you looked at her from the neck down you might guess a woman in her mid thirties. But as you moved up to her face, you would guess about sixty. Her chin receded to a double chin and her eyes bagged both above and below the slits of eyes still coated with last night's mascara. Her dyed red hair was short, sparse and curly. This morning it was especially scary. One side was matted – the other sticking out all over the place.

"What do you want?" she slurred.

"We're here to see Craig," Sydney ventured after Megan shoved her forward toward the opened door.

"Go around to the back door. It's unlocked. He's the first door on the left," she said in a monotone voice and then promptly slammed the door in their faces.

"So polite," Antoine commented. "That's why I personally voted for her firing."

The three of them headed around the house to the back door. "Does she know that?" Megan asked coyly. "Maybe she would have been more polite if we hadn't brought you along."

"I doubt that. I certainly wasn't the only vote on that one," Antoine said with a grimace and a shake of the head.

The door was indeed open. They entered and knocked on the door to the left.

No one answered the door. They began to pound louder which only brought a shout from the center of the house – "Quiet!" It was a man's voice.

They turned the knob, and the door opened. Standing in the doorway they stopped a moment to let their eyes adjust to the darkness.

The air smelled stale but then again it was a very small room. A single bed was pressed against the wall and a dresser shoved in the corner. There were clothes scattered on the floor making stepping in almost impossible.

"I don't think he's here," Megan whispered.

"Oh, yes he is," Sydney pointed to a lump huddled on the bed. "That pile can't possibly be clothing, can it?"

Antoine's face was in shock. His tidy nature was horrified at the state of the room, and he was strategically backing up into the hall and away from the mess. Megan grabbed his arm and held on for dear life. Shaking her head she clearly gave him a look that said, "Oh, no you don't!"

Sydney walked in – picking her way through the stacks of records, shoes and shirts on the floor, she managed to get to the bed. She reached down and shook Craig. With a moan he moved. First he tried to hide under the thin blanket he had on his bed. Then he squinted up shielding his eyes from the glare of the hall light.

"What are you doing here?" he asked groggily. "How did you get here?"

"Antoine, Megan and I came because we knew something was wrong when you ducked out of the meeting with that detective last night."

"What meeting? What detective?" Craig pinched his face into an even mousier expression than usual.

"Didn't you know about the meeting?" Sydney glared down at him as he rolled up to a half sitting position.

"I left right after our conversation. I didn't stick around until the end of studio hours if that's what you mean," he was now sitting up back against the wall with the blanket curled around his legs.

"So you didn't know that Darian Cooper Gray is missing?" Megan pointed a finger at him

"Missing?" He seemed at first confused. "Sure I knew she was missing. That's why I left. To find her. But guess what? She's missing!"

"Listen, I know you know a lot more about this murder than you've told anyone. We're here to collect. We need to know what you know, so stop trying to be funny. Tell us what you know. For all we know you're the murderer. It certainly isn't Richard Gray." Sydney was tired. She was tired of listening to Craig slip around the subject and

178

make leading statements that meant nothing. She was going to get to the secret he held now and that was that.

Craig wasn't smiling. "I wasn't trying to be funny. I was actually trying to find Darian… and she is missing. I'm upset about that." He hesitated and shifted his position. "I'm upset because I like Darian."

They stared at him waiting for him to continue. Megan crossed her arms and changed her weight to the other leg.

"I can't really say I'm in love with her. Craig Fritz doesn't actually ever say that he's in love with someone, now does he?" Craig was surprisingly open all of a sudden.

"Darian is a little wild. Way too wild to be married to a straight laced up tight person like Richard. He must have been a challenge for her. I can't quite figure out any other explanation for the two of them ever getting together. Anyway, Darian would tell Richard that she was out on a flight and hang out with other people like me. At first it was just a dance thing. She'd come to the clubs and hang out dancing with all the good dancers. Soon it was more than dancing between us. I didn't think much of it – I'm a one night stand kind of guy. It never bothered me that it was only that. I never said anything to Richard, and I don't think he

179

ever had a clue as to her lifestyle. It just never occurred to him to doubt her. She played him pretty good." So far Craig's explanation seemed quite plausible. Darian had seemed to be in a different world than Richard from anyone's point of view. They always seemed like black and white, day and night.

"Go on," Antoine urged. "What changed the whole thing? And what does Edward's murder have to do with this?"

Craig took a deep breath and slowly released the air. "Darian was seeing Edward as well."

Antoine's eyes narrowed. So Amanda had been right. Edward was cheating on her – and with Darian Gray. Yes, that made sense. Darian was someone that Edward couldn't have. Not only because she was already married, but because she was seeing others as well. Darian was certainly Edward's type. She was pencil thin, model like with an aloofness that challenged him.

"Go on," Antoine demanded.

"That's all," Craig shrugged his shoulders. He gave them a sly smile, "Edward and I were playing the same woman as usual. Always a contest between us. Always has been."

Sydney shook her head. That wasn't it. There was something more. Just as in their other conversations Craig was holding something back. A secret. He would say just enough but yet not all.

She grabbed his foot and yanked throwing him off balance. "Look you. I know that's not it. That's not all."

He looked startled. She had been so easy to get around. So easy to fool. It was such a delightful game for him to twist her around. Now she was demanding the rest. He looked over at the corner where his unicycle stood propped up. For all the world he wanted to jump on that cycle and pedal out the door, never having to answer this annoying woman. The two placed squarely in front of the door prevented an escape. He could try to plead ignorance, but she keep glaring at him and nagging for more.

"OK. Edward gave Darian herpes," he turned away for a moment. "That was going to stop all her fun with me. She was caught and would have to come up with some story for Richard. It would be pretty hard to hide from him." Craig stopped then added, "And she was furious."

Sydney leaned back on her heels. So the real murderer could actually be Darian Cooper Gray. "That would make sense. That would be why Richard confessed to the murder."

Craig looked strangely at her for a moment. "You know, Craig. Darian murdered Edward. That's why Richard confessed to save the one he loved."

"Or maybe he really did murder Edward just like he confessed. Darian had to tell him about the herpes and who she got it from. He went over to the office and shot him. Simple. They have the right guy after all, and it's solved." Craig's explanation hung in the air. Plausible.

"Then why would he confess after he found out Darian was pregnant? Wouldn't he want to hide it? After all, he went for long enough not saying anything. Why confess after a joyful announcement about becoming a father?" Megan popped question after question at him like a rattling gun.

"Well…," Craig hesitated. "I was upset about that little detail last night. That's why I left the studio. I couldn't figure out why she didn't tell me about that. We were together yesterday before I got to the studio. It was glorious. Especially with Edward gone, I was the man. It was a great feeling. Then you had to pop that pregnant thing on me. I

182

began to think about it. Maybe she just told Richard that she was pregnant so she wouldn't have to tell him about the herpes. Maybe it gave her an excuse or gave her a little hold over him – something to divert him from finding out about the affairs. Or then I began to think – what if it wasn't Richard's child. What if it was mine!" Craig pinched his face into disturbing look.

"Or what if it was Edward's child?" Sydney added.

They all looked at her. Craig gasped. He hadn't connected the two at all. He had been only concerned with his own involvement. His face darkened and curled into a tighter ball in the corner.

Antoine continued with the thought, "What if Darian not only found out she had herpes but also was pregnant by Edward. Not only would that ignite a confrontation with Richard and possibly end her marriage but what if Edward didn't want to be a daddy? That would leave Darian a single mom – not quite her lifestyle I'm guessing. What if Edward didn't want to end his relationship with Amanda? Would Darian kill Edward? Maybe."

Craig was looking more and more ill. His first reaction to the news about Richard's confession were getting even worse than he had first imagines. The possibilities were going in all the wrong directions.

His first thoughts had been selfishly about him and not about Edward at all.

"Just leave me alone, will you?" Craig buried his head in the blanket. "I've given you all I have. That's it. I have no more."

The three looked at each other and finally moved out into the hallway not closing the door behind them. They went out the back door and stood in a huddled clump on the driveway to discuss the matter further.

"This puts a whole new twist on the situation, doesn't it?" Antoine was shaking his head. It was painful to know he would have to break the news to Amanda about Darian. He hated to think his friend would feel betrayed by her own husband. It would be a painful day.

"We need to find Darian. That's all there is to it." Sydney began to ponder – connect the dots in her own mind.

The conversation continued for a few moments as they debated what to do next. Suddenly the back door flew open and Cutie Wilson stormed out. Her short squat body was now dressed in a pair of short shorts and a tank top that showed the sagging of her arms.

"OK, what did you do to him?" She began to screech.

The three looked at each other confused by her remark. "To whom are you referring?" Megan stated with a matter of fact air.

"Craig. He can't breathe any more. I had to call the ambulance. Did you punch him or shove him? Something's happened to him." Cutie's voice stayed at a high decibel pitch.

The three rushed past her inside to see Craig lying on his bed gasping and gray. "Do you happen to know CPR?" Antoine was saying as a medic shoved past them with Cutie now screeching at him.

They moved out to the driveway again and waited. After all Craig's room was way too small for all the people who were now rushing in and out with a stretcher. It could barely fit Craig himself.

"Looks like a collapsed lung," one medic was saying to the other as they carried him past and into the awaiting ambulance.

Cutie stood behind the three. All watched as the vehicle started its whinny alarm and pulled out to the street.

"Collapsed lung?" Megan was saying. "I don't think Craig even smoked."

"At least not cigarettes," Cutie inserted and then turned abruptly and walked back into the house.

Megan stared after Cutie then began to follow her into the house. When Sydney began to protest, Megan held up a hand to signal silence. Antoine and Sydney waited in the driveway hoping Cutie wouldn't look out the window and see them or worse yet, spot Megan in the house.

In a quick minute, Megan was out the door again and grabbing their arms for a get-away.

"What's up?" Antoine asked as he pulled away from the curb with a slight squeal of the tires.

"I got it!" Megan declared. "I got Darian's phone number. I just checked all the outgoing calls from Craig's phone during the night and copied them down. I just knew he'd have all the fancy call back gadgets to check called numbers. He'd have to with his lifestyle. One of these three numbers belongs to Darian Gray. Now just which one that would be… hmm."

Antoine quickly pulled over to a pay phone and pulled out some change. "Give me those numbers." He grabbed the paper and began to dial.

"This is Pizza Hut," he began. "Did someone order a delivery?" He waited for a response and then asked what the address was. "Sorry, I must have the wrong number on this one."

He hung up then tried again. This time his face lit up. He grabbed the pen and copied down the address. "Sorry, that isn't the address I'm looking for. I must have the number wrong. Sorry for the trouble."

He turned his back and began to mumble into the phone for a few minutes before turning back with a grin.

"I got it," he chimed as he placed the earphone back in the holder.

"We should probably turn this information over to the police immediately," Megan was saying as she passed a few more coins to Antoine.

"I suppose so," he said hesitantly. Dialing the phone, he asked for the detective who was in charge. "I see," he said. "OK. Well, I'll call back later." Then he hung up.

"He's not in. What do you want to do?"

"Well, Darian could get away. She's a flight attendant and has access to travel all over the world. I think we need to get to her before she goes anywhere else." Sydney made her pronouncement to nodding heads.

"Let's go then," Antoine slid into his seat and started up the car. "Anyone know where this is?" He passed the paper to Megan with Sydney peering over her shoulder.

"How did you get this?" Megan asked staring at the piece of paper. The name of a prominent hotel was next to the last number.

"The front desk answered and connected me to Darian's room. I asked for Darian Gray and when they didn't have her listed, I asked for Darian Cooper. Bingo. Now how do we get there?" Antoine asked again.

XXIII

Megan knew right where the hotel was located. It was just early enough for the last leg of morning congestion on the highway, so the travel was slow. At first the car was silent, but as they neared the hotel they began to formulate a plan. They couldn't very well just waltz up to Darian's room and expect she would let them in. And if she did, who's to say what she would do. She could be, after all, a cold blooded killer. Three dance teachers wouldn't stop her from somehow getting on a plane to who knows where. She certainly knew the airline system better than anyone and would know what needed to be done to escape even if the police were looking for her as a missing person.

Sydney entered the lobby first carrying Antoine's workout bag. She approached the front desk and pleasantly asked the front desk clerk for Darian Cooper's room number. "I'm her roommate and she asked me to bring her this bag before her flight out," Sydney explained with an innocent air.

Megan was already over at the line of phones calling the police, and Antoine was ready to make the call up to Darian's room. Sydney dropped the gym bag at his feet and started up the stairs to Darian's floor. She would be ready to block any attempt of escape before the police could arrive.

Antoine waited patiently for a few minutes then using the house phone dialed Darian's room number.

"Yes?" a woman answered.

Antoine tried to speak slowly without giving her time to recall who's voice was on the other end. "Just wanted to let you know that Craig has had a medical emergency this morning."

There was silence on the other end of the line. "Who is this?"

"I thought you might be interested," Antoine continued using a monotone voice.

"And why would I care?" Darian slowly answered.

"Because maybe you were having an affair with Craig." Antoine was starting to raise his voice.

"Who is this?" Darian repeated.

"We know you killed Edward Garrett. We know he gave you herpes. Did he get you pregnant as well?" By now Antoine was beginning to get more emotional.

The phone on the other end went dead. Antoine motioned for Megan to position herself in front of the elevator door to wait for Darian to try an escape. She wouldn't know at this point that the call had come from the hotel lobby. She would try to make her escape quickly.

Sydney up at the stairway door waited. She heard Darian slam her door and head toward the elevator door. Then she stopped and retraced her steps toward to the stairway exit. Sydney was ready. But as Darian open the door she spotted Sydney. Darian swung her flight carry on bag at Sydney's head. Sydney was expecting something would happen, so she ducked but in that brief moment Darian had already dropped her bag and was heading down the stairs.

Sydney followed her down hoping Antoine was ready at the bottom of the stairs. He was – ready and waiting. Darian Cooper Gray ran right into Antoine's arms just as the police pulled up to the hotel.

Megan quickly explained to the officers the events of the morning, and Darian was escorted from the hotel in handcuffs. Her pale face turned slowly to stare at the three dancers. The dark glistening hair swept across her face almost hiding a deadly glare from her dark lined eyes. Strangely dressed in a creamy white long sleeved t-shirt and white drawstring exercise pants, she was now a contrast between good and evil herself.

189

Megan, Antoine and Sydney sat down in the hotel coffee shop for donuts and coffee as they tried to sort out the fast paced morning they had just experienced.

XXIV

Antoine called Amanda from the hotel and had her meet them at the studio. The studio day would begin in an hour or so, and they would have time to fully prepare for the explanation they knew would be the center of the day.

Antoine gathered the staff in the ballroom after telling Suzanna he would be presenting the meeting. She gave him a curious look but didn't say anything in response. Her half crooked grin told him she knew something had happened, and she was interested in finding out all about why he was still dressed in jeans and t-shirt on a work day and insisting on taking over her meeting time.

As the group sat around the glass topped tables, the door clanged announcing Amanda's entrance. She was accompanied by Richard Gray and a police detective. The detective nodded at Antoine and stood back against the wall as Richard took a seat amidst hand shakes and a pat on the back from the other teachers at his release. He smiled but appeared just as curious as the rest of the group for Antoine's story.

Sydney and Megan stood up and moved their chairs behind Antoine. "Just in case I need any clarification here," Antoine explained. He began to tell the story of their morning beginning with Sydney's call asking for a ride and ending with Darian's arrest at the hotel. Richard moved back and forth in his chair uncomfortably as Antoine told of their conversation with Craig and his admission of Darian's affairs with both Edward and Craig. Richard buried his head in his hands when Antoine told of the herpes and pregnancy speculation.

The detective stepped forward after the story was complete and cleared his throat. "As difficult as it is for you, Richard to hear this side of the story, I would just like to confirm that we had been in contact with Darian's doctor and yes, she did have herpes. The pregnancy has also been confirmed and tests have shown that the father is in fact Edward. Darian had the tests already completed before she presented Edward with the facts. She wanted a trump card before she demanded he divorce Amanda and marry her. Edward was not as joyful as she had hoped. In fact he shredded the test results in front of her to show how supportive he was of her plan. He told her to get out and never show her face in the studio again. With no support from Edward, she felt her only recourse was to kill him and try to pull the same plan on Craig. Craig would be easier. He wouldn't demand proof of paternity with Edward gone. Unfortunately, Mr. Gray here also believed he was the father and when he discovered that Darian was involved with Edward Garrett, he knew who had murdered the man. Darian's car in the garage was further evidence that he could use to put the blame on himself and save Darian from prison. Unfortunately for Darian, you Mr. Gray have some very good friends who believed in your innocence. And although we don't condone interference in police matters, we are certainly grateful that these friends of yours decided to dig a little deeper. Good luck to all of you, and we will be in touch for any further interviews that will certainly be needed to conclude this case."

The detective left and the teachers moved their chairs a little closer together. Richard no longer sat in his normal upright erect position and Amanda was tucked into Antoine's arms. Suzanna had separated herself briefly from the group to put on a slow quiet Bolero to drown out the silence. After a few moments she spoke.

"This has been a trying time for all of us. But we have continued, and we have supported each other as best we knew how. Richard, we certainly welcome you back with the staff if you feel you would like to return." She paused, waiting for an answer.

"This has been so overwhelming. I have a rather bad taste in my mouth for the studio at this moment, although I appreciate all of you who stood by me through this ordeal. I will have to give this some thought as to what I will do after today. All I can think about right now is how to get through today." Richard straightened and his stone faced expression softened for a brief moment.

Amanda spoke, "This is very difficult for many of us." She turned toward Richard. "I feel the pain you are feeling. I also know that knowledge is relief. I have mourned for the past few weeks and am ready to move on to some extent." She turned to Suzanna. "I would like to offer you half of the studio Suzanna. I know that it means much more to you than to me. I would like to continue to use the studio for my exercise program. Like Edward, I too know that if I'm not in shape, my career will not continue. And my career will be a comfort to me at this point." Turning to Antoine she began, "I don't know how to thank all of my friends here at the studio for all you have done. Thanks." And she was silent.

192

"So what will we do with Terry when he returns?" Suzanna clapped her hands and turned to the group. "Do we give him a second chance? What do you all feel about that situation?"

After a few moments of discussion, they agreed that as uncomfortable as Terry made them, they needed to give him a chance to redeem himself. But everyone knew they would be on guard when he was around – a little more careful. The door clanged.

Mimi giggled and clopped across the floor in her high heeled mules to give Richard a huge hug. Her face was heavily made up but no traces of the bruising could be seen under flesh toned coloring. Her hair looked freshly teased with a headband scarf around the forehead.

"How are you honey?" she screeched in her high pitched voice.

Richard blushed and smiled. "How are you honey?" he retorted back.

"Actually, I'm doing great!" she reported. "The police picked up my ex, and he is in jail awaiting trial for battery. He'll probably be out in a few months but that will give me time to get my life in order and find a new place that will be safe. I'm ready." She gave Richard another hug then went around the circle.

Morgan walked around to the desk to get the appointment sheet for the day. "This place is too much. Drama, drama, drama. Wouldn't miss a day… Ok, who is going to teach whom?" She demanded looking from Suzanna to Antoine. "Let's get this day settled now."

Several of the teachers had moved to the center of the floor and were dancing a slow Bolero. Calm and collected. Life went on.

www.ingramcontent.com/pod-product-compliance
Lightning Source LLC
Chambersburg PA
CBHW061202170626
46809CB00003B/1204